When You Kiss Me

MELINDA CURTIS

Dedication

To Mr. Curtis, for his belief in fate. For this, he can be forgiven his boredom with Shakespeare.

~

Reader Bonus

Head out to Melinda's website (MelindaCurtis.com) and look for the signup button to receive her newsletter and receive free reads.

Prologue

DOROTHY SUMMER COULDN'T UNDERSTAND YOUNG people nowadays.

Or at least, those in their twenties and thirties who seemed adrift, wondering what to do with their lives. They wanted fortune. Or they wanted fame. But they didn't seem to have any idea what to do to earn fame or fortune, or, more importantly, how to satisfy their soul.

Dotty, on the other hand, did. She had a bucket list, and, by golly, this seasoned widow was going to spend her days checking things off. She'd already made good on several items, including driving an air boat through the Everglades, dating a younger man, and singing a Broadway tune with one of its stars.

She had some of her granddaughters to thank for that, specifically, the daughters of her son Tim. Those five young women weren't tempted by fame or fortune. They had purpose when it came to their careers. Kitty, the doctor. Maggie, the veterinarian. Lily, the state politician. Aubrey, the botanist. Violet, the literature professor. If only one of them would give her a great-grandchild. When Dotty was older and less mobile, she wouldn't mind sitting and rocking a little one.

But before that, there was her bucket list. And currently on the top of that list was being a model for a famous designer.

And that was why Dotty was following fashion designer Xuri out of Lily's engagement party and into the gardens of Tim's Hamptons property. She was on a first name basis with the designer because of private showings. "Xuri, do you have a moment?"

The elegant young woman stopped and executed a runway pivot that her fashion models would have envied. She wore a pair of baggy black and white striped pants with a super-skimpy top—what looked like a Bedazzled bullet bra. *So daring!* Hoop earrings the diameter of a mixing bowl hung from her ears. She had short purple hair that was in the spiky bed-head style young folks seemed to favor. And her expression was haughty. In fact, Xuri seemed poised to yell, *"Off with their heads!"*

Dotty fingered the traditional string of pearls around her neck. "Are you hiring? Models, that is." All Dotty's life, she'd had more luck cutting through, than beating around, the bush. "I have the body type you're looking for." Dress size two. Dotty struck a pose. Too bad she was no taller than a horseracing jockey. Runway models tended to be much taller.

"You would model for me?" Xuri asked in her formal, slightly accented speech. Her eyebrows were sprinkled with tiny dots of silver glitter. She waggled them in what Dotty thought was amusement, sparkles catching the Hampton afternoon sunlight like moonbeams on cresting ocean waves.

"I would." Dotty came closer, feeling overdressed in her party attire. "Your winter coat collection was fabulous this year. And the way the models came down the runway during Fashion Week was so fun." They hadn't strutted. They'd bopped.

That praise earned Dotty a small smile, seemingly reluctantly given. "My models are dancers first."

"I can bust a move with the best of them." And to prove it, Dotty struck another pose, this one from Michael Jackson's

Thriller video. She thrust her hips forward and back so hard her lower back twinged, causing her to spasm. "*I-eee-eee!*"

Xuri reached out a hand to steady Dotty, numerous brass bracelets bangling. "You have moves. But my dancers do hip hop."

"I can hip hop." Dotty had no idea what hip hop was. But she was determined to learn.

Xuri's sparkly brows caught the sunlight again, practically blinding Dotty this time. "I will send you a coat."

"And I will learn hip hop," Dotty said gleefully. "Please send the coat here as I'm spending the next few weeks here with my granddaughter."

A white horse galloped past, nearly as blinding as Xuri's eyebrows since it had no halter, bridle, or saddle to mar its snowy appearance.

They both stared at the riderless horse for a moment, it not being a usual sight in the Hamptons.

"We need to make a wish," Dotty told Xuri as the horse galloped across the backyard toward the ocean. "White horses are a sign of good luck. Like a four leaf clover or a rainbow."

"I wish you good health." Xuri returned to the party, black and white striped pants billowing in the ocean breeze. She paused at the door to call over her shoulder, "And I will send you a coat!"

Chapter One

PROFESSOR VIOLET SUMMER WAS HAPPY WITH THE direction of her life.

When she told that to her younger sister Maggie, who was a jilted bride, Maggie laughed.

They were behind their parents' Hamptons house where their sister Lily's engagement party was being held. They walked toward the beach, each with a drink in hand. Maggie held a bottle of beer. Violet held a glass of sauvignon blanc. They sat down in the sand and stared at the ocean, squinting in the summer afternoon sun.

"How can you be happy? We're the last two single sisters standing." Maggie sipped her beer, short black hair tousled by the ocean breeze. "We need to find men and soon, regardless of whether or not we've been burned and broken-hearted in the past."

"Count me out. I'm up for tenure this year at Harvard," Vi told her. She'd climbed the ladder from assistant to associate professor over the course of six years. And now, a full professorship was within reach in year seven. "I have classes to plan for, academic papers to write, and a book on Shakespeare to publish."

A book she needed to finish this summer. "If I don't make tenure, I'll be let go."

Every waking moment needed to be devoted to achieving a permanent position at the prestigious university. Vi's entire identity was now wrapped up in the endeavor.

"My short-term goals aren't so lofty. I'm looking for a man to take to Kitty's wedding." Maggie removed her sandals and pushed her bare feet in the sand. "You know her engagement to Beck is inevitable. And since I used to be engaged to Beck, my date needs to be someone *extra*."

"I can't argue with that." Vi sipped her wine as a particularly loud wave crashed on the shore, thinking it wouldn't be so bad to attend another Summer family event dateless. The afternoon heat beat down on her. Vi tugged her blue silk tank top away from her damp back and smoothed out the wrinkles in her sand-colored linen slacks, wishing she wore cotton shorts and a T-shirt. And then she looked at her youngest sister. "What do you mean by *extra*?"

"I don't know. Rich, handsome...maybe even royal." Maggie laughed. "That's it. I want my own crown-wearing Prince Charming."

Yikes. Although Vi understood the need for Maggie to bolster her courage during Kitty's nuptials, which were very much likely to happen, Maggie was setting the bar extremely high and was likely to be disappointed. Vi didn't want her to experience more upset.

"A real prince? Those are rare, Mags. We get one or two at Harvard. But very few and from such small kingdoms that a royal title seems a bit sketchy." The last thing Maggie needed was a sketchy guy in her life.

"You've met a prince? Get out." Maggie bumped her shoulder playfully against Violet's, fixating on the wrong thing. "Can you introduce me?"

Double yikes. Violet wanted her sister to be happy, but not at the expense of tenure.

"No, Mags. I can't afford to do anything that will look bad to the review committee." Violet had to have a squeaky-clean reputation both on and off campus.

"Come on. One prince. For me. *Please?*" Maggie set her beer in the sand, laced her fingers, and propped her chin on her digits. She blinked her big eyes at Vi.

"Well..." Violet was close to her sisters and wanted them to be happy, especially Maggie, who'd had a difficult year or so. "I can't do anything until I get tenure. So, you better hope Kitty's wedding is in the distant future."

Maggie threw her arms around Vi. "I knew you'd find me a prince!"

"Excuse me, ladies." A cowboy appeared in front of them. His tan cowboy boots were buried nearly to his ankles in the sand. He was tall, muscular, and wore a wide-brimmed black hat. "Have you seen a white horse?"

Violet blinked. She leaned closer to Maggie. "I think I've had too much to drink. I'm seeing things. Specifically, a tall, sexy cowboy with kissable lips."

Said cowboy apparition grinned as if he'd heard her.

Maggie shaded her eyes with one hand. "I'm seeing the same mirage. But it's got to be a hallucination. We don't get cowboys in the Hamptons. Now, if he was a polo player..."

Horse hooves thundered toward them from behind.

"Never mind, ladies. I see her." The cowboy walked past them and whistled shrilly, then called, "*Tally-ho!*"

"I'm so confused. Now the cowboy is calling out the fox hunt?" Violet was afraid to turn around and look, because if he wasn't there, someone had spiked her wine *and* Maggie's beer.

"It's no mirage, Vi." Maggie shoved her feet in her sandals and stood, helping Violet to her feet.

They both turned just as a white horse skidded to a halt, practically landing on its haunches, and sending a wave of sand toward Violet and Maggie.

The cowboy didn't move a muscle other than to hold out an apple slice. "Good girl, Tally. Easy now."

The mare's pink nostrils flared. Refusing the treat, she jerked her head to look at Vi and Maggie, flanks heaving as if she'd run much more than she was used to.

"You want a slice of apple, don't you, girl," the cowboy said in a sultry voice that tugged at something deep in Violet's chest, something she'd locked away during her first year at Harvard. "You want it more than you want to trample me or these pretty ladies."

Violet gasped. Unlike Maggie, who was a big animal veterinarian, Vi wasn't used to being around anything larger than a golden retriever. And trampling...

"I'm just kidding." The cowboy gave Vi a look over his shoulder that made her pulse beat like castanets in experienced fingers. "Tally's as gentle as a kitten, aren't you, honey?" His voice was deep and rich with a slight Texas twang. And just listening to it made Vi think of long, slow kisses on cold winter nights.

The mare took a step closer to the cowboy, then another. She heaved a sigh as if giving in to the inevitable, to this cowboy, to this man, to the idea of his kiss.

And Violet had definitely had too much to drink because that cowboy called to her the same way he called to that horse of his. She took a step closer. And then another.

In one smooth movement, the cowboy leapt onto the mare's back—no saddle, no reins, no halter.

"*Oh.*" Violet's knees went weak. He was hot, hotter than Lily's fiancé, actor Judson Hambly. "*Oh,*" Vi said again but dreamily this time because it seemed required. Everything about the man was larger than life. For the past six years, men in her life were mostly limited to Shakespearean heroes who leaped off the page in her dreams or poorly produced movies.

"Thanks for your help, ma'ams." The cowboy extended a hand toward Vi, as if for a shake.

Violet eyed that hand. Handshakes were rarer now that the world had been through a pandemic. "I didn't do anything."

"You didn't run screaming, which would have made Tally bolt to Sag Harbor." His hand still hung in the air between them.

Vi took it, momentarily losing herself in his large clasp and the heat of his skin.

Such a firm grip.

It said he was decisive and sure of himself. Vi liked confidence in a man, as long as he wasn't overly-confident and cocky and didn't take her on newsworthy adventures.

"To properly thank you, let's go for a ride." Without warning, the cowboy swung Violet up behind him, let out one of those enthusiastic cowboy cries, and then sent the horse galloped across the beach.

Leaving Violet's wine and her sister behind them.

~

CHARLES COOPER PEARSON THE THIRD was having a good day.

For the past few months, good days were rare.

He'd been disowned and cut off by his father. For the first time in his thirty-five years, Coop had no silver spoon to fall back on. He'd had to find work and a place to live. He'd had to find a place in the world and eke out a living without benefit of the Pearson name and resources. Most days, it sucked.

But today, he'd found a horse worthy of his talents in the Hamptons. Or at least, a horse that liked listening to him. Okay, Tally didn't completely listen to him. In fact, the mare thought she was the boss in their relationship.

But once he'd found Tally after she'd escaped, the white mare had helped him with an introduction to a woman who was currently hanging onto him for dear life, shouting in his ear, and smelling like a patch of sweet wildflowers.

Best. Day. Ever.

Coop whooped.

He pressed one arm over the woman's hands on his waist to help keep her safe behind him as he guided Tally with a combination of leg pressure and a twist of her mane.

"Have you lost your mind?" the woman behind him cried as they galloped in the surf, water splashing around them.

He laughed. This was the best he'd felt since he'd been banished from Houston two months ago.

His old man would say he was living too much in the moment without thinking about the responsibilities of the future.

You'd be wrong, old man.

Coop *was* thinking about the future. About galloping down the beach until he reached a private dock. About riding up the bank and beneath the shady line of trees that led to Beeswax Farm. About how the pretty woman behind him would catch her breath and admire the scenery instead of focusing on her fear. About how her smile would return when both their feet were on solid ground, and she'd realize how unforgettable riding on a whim would be. About him leaning down and tasting those sweet red lips of hers.

Coop slowed the mare as he came even with the dock and made the turn toward the farm.

"Thank heavens," the brunette breathed into his ear.

See? She was calming down already.

Tally trotted up the rise and beneath the trees. Coop cued her into a walk.

And unable to resist, he eased his torso around and made a play for those tantalizing lips.

"Not so fast." His passenger unexpectedly slid off the back of the horse, landing without falling on her behind, but just barely.

Coop cued Tally in a circle, until he faced his wildflower woman. He took another good, hard look at her.

She had long brown hair that would never fall smooth as silk. It was thick and wavy, the kind of hair a man's hand could get tangled in during a long kiss. Her eyes were big and brown and expressive. Before he'd swung her up behind him, those eyes had been game for an adventure. Now they flashed a warning. Her red lips were full and made for smiling, not that frown. She was dressed for one of those parties Hampton folk liked so much—pants a soft tan and a mess of wrinkles, a cream-colored blouse that hadn't fared much better from being pressed against him. And her pretty face...

Brows lowered, she was itching for a fight, and he refused to let her fire the first salvo.

"I hope you weren't expecting a refund," Coop said instead of apologizing like his mama would have wanted.

"A refund? For what?"

"*A ride that dreams are made of.*" It was a modification of a quote from Shakespeare. Sappy, but it fit the moment.

Dad would be so proud.

Charles Cooper Pearson the Second may have been an oil man, but Dad loved him some Shakespeare. Although Coop's father would never condone using Mr. Shakespeare's words as a pick-up. And maybe, for the most part, he'd be right. However, using Shakespeare's words had become second nature to Coop. Not that Coop relied on the old bard's quotes to win women. No. He used his patented smile for that, bringing it into play after a woman laughed off his Shakespearean-based lines.

Although...

The target of his intentions didn't burst out laughing at his words. Or dress him down for being a jerk with a too-cheesy line. Instead, she narrowed her eyes and said sharply, "*What did you say?*"

"*A ride that dreams are made of.*" He spoke slowly, tipping his hat back and leaning forward, grinning, to make sure she got the message: *I'm attracted to you, honey.*

And she to him. She'd said he looked kissable when he'd first come upon her at the beach.

Whether they did something about that attraction was another matter.

"*All that glitters is not gold.*" She shook her head, tossing a more accurate Shakespearean quote back at him, which was intellectual hotness.

No one ever caught on to his use of Shakespeare, much less gorgeous women who smelled of bluebonnet-strewn fields and didn't fall off on impromptu bareback rides.

She waved a hand as if brushing him aside. "I'm going to give you a pass for what just happened, Shakespeare. It was all my fault, after all. I trusted you with my hand."

"So gracious." He hadn't expected that of her. And yet, she was also somehow cynical. Neither of which took the sting out of her rejection. *Women never rejected Coop!*

"You should be careful who you offer rides to out here," she told him in a voice he imagined kindergarten teachers used on misbehaving five year-olds, soft yet unyielding. "Some women are more particular than the likes of me when it comes to the treatment of wardrobe, hair, and manicures."

She was anything but *some women*. She was special. He knew that instinctively. "Noted, Miss..."

His Hamptons beauty shook her head a little, smiling. "You have a nice day, Shakespeare. Give Tally some oats." She turned, making her way down the bank to the beach in her impractical sandals.

And for the first time since his father had kicked him to the curb, Coop wanted to follow more than a whim.

He wanted to follow her.

Chapter Two

THAT COWBOY...

Back at her parents' house, Violet slipped into the kitchen, registering the hum of voices that indicated her twin sister Lily's engagement party had wound down but wasn't quite finished. She hurried up the rear staircase.

She didn't want to answer questions about where she'd been. What would she say if asked? Tenured Harvard professors didn't participate in impromptu escapades. And yet, she was hard-pressed to get the bold, Shakespearean cowboy out of her mind.

Talk about fantasies fulfilled.

A scholarly cowboy in the Hamptons?

Le Sigh.

No. No-no-no. There will be no sighing. And no distracting thoughts about what might have been if she'd let him kiss her either.

Self-lecture complete, Violet opened the door to her bedroom, startling Maggie from what looked like a nap on her yellow rose coverlet. "What are you doing here?"

"Waiting for you." Maggie sat up and yawned. She'd changed into black leggings and a tank top. "I thought you'd be gone longer. Did the cowboy bring you back? I hope you got his number. He was hot."

"No number. And I walked back." Violet shed her wrinkled clothes, changing into shorts and a maroon Harvard T-shirt. "He's trouble. I can tell."

"He's an adventure," Maggie countered. "Something you haven't had in a long time. Don't you miss being impulsive and reckless? I used to be so envious of your life."

"The last time I was impulsive and reckless, I was lectured by my dean about how Harvard staff represent Harvard at all times." She'd been dating a NASCAR driver and their appearance at the Burning Man event had made headlines. That had been during the first few months of her employment and Violet had stopped acting like an heiress then and there. In fact, she'd started completely buying into the role of distinguished Harvard professor. "Someday, after I receive tenure, I'm going to settle down with a nice man. Until then, there will be no escapades."

But the way my cowboy looked at me...

Like she hadn't changed at all. Like she was still game for adventures with scoundrels and kisses stolen by strangers.

"I can't be distracted." Violet dug her laptop out of its bag and sat on the bed next to Maggie.

"Are you creating a social media post?" Maggie flopped back on the bed. "About how you were whisked away by Cowboy Hunky?"

"No. I'm adding to my research notes." She suddenly felt inspired. Her cowboy kidnapping was an example of how fate, something William Shakespeare had thought couldn't be avoided, could in fact be thwarted with positive results, unlike many of the bard's plays.

My cowboy.

Violet rolled her eyes.

The bedroom door burst open. "Who knows how to dance the hip hop? I need to learn." Grandma Dotty closed the door furtively behind her. She strutted forward, waving her petite arms, and shaking her practically non-existent booty. "And don't tell your father. If he had his way, I'd be knitting in a corner room of a retirement facility."

Maggie and Violet exchanged glances. Grandma Dotty had been battling the onset of dementia for the past couple of years. The doctors adjusted her meds every few months, which meant that sometimes Grandma Dotty was clear as a bell. And other times? She got a bit frenetic and obsessed with things on her bucket list. This seemed like one of the latter times.

"Why the sudden interest in hip hop?" Violet asked tentatively. Her grandmother was never direct about her motives, and this smacked of trouble.

"Let's just say it's an interest of mine." Grandma Dotty held her arms up, bent at the elbows like a goal post. She opened and closed her arms as if they were a set of imaginary doors. "*Ready or not. Here I come,*" she sang a line from a Fugees song in a warbly, high-pitched voice.

"That's not a hip hop song," Violet murmured.

"I think there's a hip hop class weekday mornings down at the Pilates studio by the gelato place." Maggie had no filter, even when she hadn't been drinking.

Violet poked her sister's leg. "Don't encourage this. Are you going to take her?" Maggie may live and work in another part of the Hamptons, but it was Vi who was staying in this house for the summer and on Grandma Dotty watch. The rest of the family was heading back to New York tonight.

"No. In addition to office hours, I'm on call all week." Maggie brushed Violet's hand away. She worked as a veterinarian at a large animal practice. "But you should go with Grandma Dotty to hip hop cardio. Sitting and studying those dusty old books all day can't be good for you."

"I'm finishing a book." Vi thought longingly of her topic— Shakespeare's understanding of the human condition. The man's words were as applicable today as when they'd been written several hundred years ago. "And my deadline is looming."

"*No diggity.*" Changing records, Grandma Dotty crab walked sideways across the floor on two legs. Then she spun around and shook her skinny butt back-and-forth at them.

"Grandma Dotty, have you been drinking?" Vi set her laptop aside and stood, turning her grandmother around so she could look her in the eye.

Both eyes were clear and filled with sparks of mischief. She shook her head. "No drinks other than a toast. I've been given an opportunity to model for Xuri. Except I need to learn hip hop."

Maggie and Vi exchanged glances again. And then they started to laugh.

There was no way the trendy, Pan Asian fashion designer was going to let their white-as-snow grandmother walk—*or hip hop*—down her runway.

Grandma Dotty crossed her arms over her chest and sniffed her disdain. "You'll believe me when Xuri sends me a coat for my audition."

Violet tried hard to keep a straight face. "If Xuri sends you a coat, I'll take you to hip hop cardio every day this summer."

"You'll take me anyway." Grandma Dotty struck a coy pose. "Because we're housemates and you love me."

～

"THIS IS what happens when you teach horses dog tricks, Chuck." Rafi snorted as he pushed the wheelbarrow full of stall waste out of the main barn and past an incoming Coop.

"You're just upset because Tally is smarter than you are." Coop led the white mare back to her stall with a hand on her neck, fingers wrapped around a handful of coarse mane.

"Chuck, Chuck, Chuck." Rafi took great pleasure in saying Coop's alias. Not that the live-in farm manager knew it was an alias. He assumed Coop was just another down-on-his-luck cowboy happy to exercise horses for a daily wage. "I'm not the one who let a horse escape, Chuckaroo. You can't make too many more mistakes like that with expensive horse flesh, or you'll be out a job. And then who will Chuck-Chuck have to talk to?"

Normally, Coop let Rafi's teasing roll over him. But today, after things didn't go as expected with the brunette, Coop was feeling every slight and not open to his supervisor's glib cautionary notes.

He was Charles Cooper Pearson the Third, for cryin' out loud! Heir to a massive oil fortune in Texas. Or at least, he had been until his father had a heart attack two months ago.

"I've made mistakes, Cooper." His father had clung to Coop's hand from his hospital bed, looking pale, frail and afraid. "And I can correct them. Starting with you."

"*Me*?" Coop would've taken a step back if his father's grip hadn't suddenly turned strong. "Shouldn't you start by eating better and reducing your workload?"

"That's it exactly. You can't take any of my workload." Dad's bedside cardiac machine beeped faster. "Your office has cobwebs. Life is one big party to you. Fast cars. Fast women. A fast way to the ruin of everything our family has built. But no more!"

Coop tried to calm his old man, focusing his counter-argument on the point pertinent to the situation. "You haven't needed me at the office. When I show up, you don't let me do anything." Nothing but tag along to meetings like an unwanted growth. It was part of the reason why Coop stayed away. The other reason being that he and his father were cut from the same cloth. Both wanted to be in charge rather than a second or third—or not even a little bit—in command.

"What can I trust you with? *Huh*?" His father's face was turning red. The beeps on the machine he was hooked up to increased in intensity. Alarms sounded somewhere down the hall. "You will go away for three months. Tell none of your friends or the rest of the family where you're going. Tell no one who you are."

"Go away? Now?" When Coop's father might actually need him? "Dad, you're not making sense."

Footsteps pounded in the hallway, fast approaching.

"Leave your credit and bank cards," Dad wheezed. "Leave your cars, your electronics, and your clothes."

"You're cutting me off?" Coop went numb. "Okay, you can do that. Just...just don't send me away now." *When you might be dying.*

His father clung to Coop's hand. "Leave. Find your gift. Fate knows the way."

"My gift?" *Fate?* "Dad... No." No on so many levels.

No, don't die!

No, don't send me away!

And lastly, selfishly...*No, don't be disappointed in me!*

It was true that Coop had spent the last five years living what might from the outside seem like an aimless life. Unwanted at his family business, Coop had taken advantage of his trust fund and worked gratis at several start-ups in Texas, gaining all kinds of experience in solving business problems. If Dad was going to need time to recover from this set-back, Coop was ready to fill his shoes.

"No," Coop said again, louder this time. "You need me."

"I don't," Dad insisted, pitching his hoarse voice lower still, "Not yet. *Like madness is the glory of this life.*"

Coop identified the words as those of Shakespeare. His father loved Shakespeare and quoted him embarrassingly often. But Coop had no idea what his old man was talking about this time.

"Talk to Stratton about the next 90 days," Dad wheezed as Coop was pushed out of the way and then out of the room, where his father's assistant had plucked Coop's wallet from his pocket, removed his credit cards, and then asked for his cell phone, house and truck keys.

All of which Coop had numbly handed over while he waited to make sure his father was still alive.

I'm still waiting.

Coop hadn't heard from his father in two months. Pride kept him from calling home or searching for family news on the internet. After doing odd jobs for cash and hitchhiking halfway across the United States, he'd ended up in the Hamptons, landed some odd jobs, and a closet of a room to sleep in. Only then had he bought a cheap cell phone. Only then had he looked up the meaning of that last quote—*Like madness is the glory of this life.* It had some reference to over-spending leading to bankruptcy. But that was the literal meaning. The internet was full of hidden meanings and symbolic translations. Shakespeare's words could be bent to any meaning you wanted.

What had his father been trying to tell him?

And what if Coop's Hamptons princess who'd quoted Shakespeare back at him knew or had some insight about it?

Coop rolled his eyes.

I'm reaching for straws now.

"Chuck," Rafi said again in the here-and-now. He stood near the tack room. "Will you come work for me when I have my own horse farm?"

"When will that be?" Coop asked instead of bolstering Rafi's dream the way he usually would.

"When I win the lottery." Rafi's laugh was a bit sad. "Banks, man. They don't lend money to people with nothing more in their account than dreams."

"Someday, you'll meet a banker who believes in you," Coop told him, hoping that was true. The world could be unfair. Coop had been born with the resources to pursue a dream. Why couldn't Rafi be afforded the same chance?

"Someday might just as easily be never." Rafi shook his head ruefully. "Are you driving tonight?"

"Yeah." Coop drove for a local private car service, as did Rafi. It took two jobs to make ends meet in the Hamptons and driving a Town Car paid more than driving for Uber or Lyft. Even so, Coop's standard of living was barely an existence compared to his old way of life. "How about you? Are you driving tonight?"

"Nope. I have a date." Rafi tilted his straw cowboy hat at a jaunty angle. "Unlike you, Chuck, I have plans for my future. Become a renowned horse trainer with my own horse farm, find a girl, settle down. Not necessarily in that order."

"The future..." Coop scoffed.

He couldn't plan beyond the next thirty days.

Chapter Three

"I'M READY FOR HIP HOP CARDIO." GRANDMA DOTTY burst into Violet's room at *oh-no-you-did-not-wake-me-up* thirty. She wore baggy shorts, a man's blue-checked button-down, and high top sneakers. She'd spiked her gray hair in a mohawk. "Let's get zesty."

"I think the word you're looking for is *spicy*." Violet stretched. "Did Xuri's coat arrive?"

"No. Not yet."

"Wake me when it does." Violet pulled the covers over her head. She wasn't a morning person. "That was our deal."

"Come on, Vi. It starts at seven." Grandma Dotty climbed on the mattress and bounced up-and-down. "You know it'll be fun. You loved to dance when we were at that wedding in Ecuador."

"We were ballroom dancing." And it had been at a decent hour.

Her grandmother stopped bouncing. "*Please.*"

"Can't. There are no cars here." Her family had left last night, including Maggie, who worked and lived in nearby Bridgehampton. It was just Vi and Dotty in the house. "Remember that I don't own a car anymore." She didn't need one in Cambridge.

"Oh." Grandma Dotty seemed surprised. "I forgot. I'll call the service. The number is on the fridge."

"Yikes. Really? Don't..." Violet sat up. But Grandma Dotty had already left the room. "I wanted to work all day." Violet flopped back in bed.

What were the odds that she'd get any work done if Grandma Dotty didn't get to her hip hop class this morning?

Slim to none.

Vi had to go.

Twenty minutes later, Violet was downstairs dressed in leggings, a sports bra, yellow sneakers, and a tank top that read, "*Nerds have all the fun.*" She carried her phone and purse and was just locking up when a black Lincoln Town Car pulled in the long, circular driveway. She sighed. "Couldn't we just Uber?"

The black car was old school and said stodgy old money rode inside.

"You know that *I* don't know how to app anything." Grandma Dotty fidgeted on the step next to her and then got distracted by a row of blooming yellow roses. "I dial, Vi. Don't try to change me." She wandered along the flower bed.

Meanwhile, the driver hopped out and came around to open the door for them.

The driver...

Vi gasped.

The driver should have worn a cowboy hat and blue jeans, not a cheap black suit and tie.

"*You.*" Never a morning person, Violet's bad mood worsened.

Shakespeare grinned. "You live here?"

"No." Violet's guard came up. She'd been burned before by men who saw her for the money she'd inherit someday rather than the woman who stood before them. "I'm just here as my grandmother's companion." There. She sounded like a poor relation. "Let's go, grandma."

Grandma Dotty quit smelling the roses and trotted over.

Her—*the*—cowboy chauffeur nodded toward her grandmother. "Good morning. I'm told you're heading into town for a workout."

"Don't shake his hand, Grandma," Violet said in a cool voice. "You might end up somewhere else entirely."

"But you'd enjoy it." That grin. He had no trouble keeping it up.

Grandma Dotty blinked at Violet. "You know him?"

"In passing." Vi sniffed.

"It's fate." The chauffeuring cowboy placed a hand over his heart. "*What must be, must be.*"

"And now you're quoting Romeo and Juliet?" Violet tried to keep up the charade that he was annoying, but...*be still my heart.* Shakespeare's words had crossed those perfect lips of his twice in as many days.

"Shakespeare? He's just your type, Vi." Grandma Dotty applauded. "Not to mention, he's easy to look at and punctual."

Vi rolled her eyes. "Don't encourage him."

"Vi?" Shakespeare's dark eyebrows rose. "Short for..."

"Violet." Grandma Dotty climbed in the back and scooted across to make room for Vi.

"*Violet?*" Shakespeare scoffed. "She's no shrinking flower. She's too vivid. She's a...a...a...*Vivi.* That's double the intensity of a violet." The way he said it, with such certainty, was like a proclamation.

Violet sat next to her grandmother, staring up at the charmer holding her car door and trying hard not to fall under his spell. "Nicknames can only be given by friends or family."

The implication being he was neither.

"But we should be friends. I'm..." He hesitated, looking disappointed for some reason. His fingers clenched on the car door. "I'm Chuck, friend to Vivi and her grandmother."

His name is Chuck?

Heroes were never named Chuck. Nor did Chucks spout Shakespeare.

"I'm Dot to-the-E, professional hip hop dancer to be. Dotty

Summer." Grandma Dotty was loving this. She grinned from ear-to-ear. "Make sure we ride to the right kind of tunes to get ready for hip hop cardio, Chuck."

Violet groaned.

"Guaranteed." Shakespeare—not Chuck, *never Chuck*—closed the car door and strode around the front of the car to get in. "Hip hop cardio, here we come."

Violet rubbed a hand over her forehead. "Just what I need. An enabler."

"Enabler?" Shakespeare tsked. "I make women happy."

"I bet you do," Vi said, heavy on the sarcasm. "Sweeping them off their feet and galloping into the sunset."

"And if I'm lucky, stopping for a kiss." Chuck's gaze caught hers, such a clear brown.

Violet's breath caught. Those eyes... Those cheekbones... He had a full head of hair with a small cowlick at his crown. Straight white teeth. Lips with a tendency to smile. And kiss. Those lips would definitely do a lot of great kissing.

Violet caught herself before she spent time dwelling upon his hands. "Geez, I should have had coffee this morning." Maybe then she wouldn't be fantasizing about kissing a guy who already took too many liberties.

He took no liberties with his core workout.

Those abs were amazing. They'd been firm as she'd gripped his waist on that horseback ride.

Violet caught herself again.

I am above this.

She'd outgrown the need for adventures and escapades.

If I'd have known he was our driver, I'd have had a Bloody Mary for breakfast to take the edge off.

Shakespeare did a horrible job of suppressing a laugh, earning a hard stare from Violet.

"What are you mumbling about?" Grandma Dotty was practicing her arm moves, which consisted of cross-body reaches and snaps. "Did you say something about Mary? Do I know

Mary? Was she at the party yesterday? Does she do hip hop cardio?"

"Did I say that out loud?" *Lovely.* Sleep deprivation had removed Violet's filter.

Shakespeare didn't even try to hold back the laughter this time.

Grrr. Vi needed distance between herself and this man. And in her experience, the best way to deter a man was with a little snark. "Grandma Dotty, I don't think Chuck looks like a Chuck. Isn't he more like a Chas or a Chip?" He may dress like the help, but he had a million-dollar smile.

And score! Her comment wiped the smile from Shakespeare's overly-handsome face. Maybe now she could resist his magnetism.

"Now, Vi. It's not nice to tease a hard-working man like Chuck."

"*Work more than other,*" he muttered what sounded like another Shakespeare quote.

"Don't play that card," Violet said, girding herself against the idea that not-Chuck was a unicorn in the forest of sports statistic-touting men.

"What card?" Oh, he was trying to play dumb.

But Violet wasn't buying it. He was too sharp to be a stable boy/limo driver. If they'd been in Hollywood, she would have assumed he was an aspiring scriptwriter with a degree from UCLA film school. But here... Here he could be anything. The question was what. An over-educated dot com flop? A down on his luck investment banker? A wannabe entrepreneur looking for financing?

"Vi doesn't joke about Shakespeare." Grandma Dotty played corners, leaning into Violet as their driver made a left turn a little too fast. "It's her gift. Her life's work."

"Her *gift?*" Shakespeare glanced at Violet in the rear view mirror without a tease or that devilish grin of his. That glance gave importance to her so-called gift and gave Violet pause to consider a more serious side of him.

Grandma Dotty nodded. "Vi's going to spend the rest of summer working on a book on Shakespeare, from morning to night. That leaves no time for anything but hip hop cardio and dinner with me at The Palm."

One of the most expensive restaurants in East Hampton and not a nightly destination as far as Violet's wallet was concerned. She may be an heiress, but she had yet to inherit anything.

"Are we there yet?" Violet asked, not entirely sure where they were going. There were dozens of small exercise studios in the Hamptons that provided yoga, Pilates, and cardio workouts.

"We're here." Shakespeare double parked and ran around to open Grandma Dotty's door. "And listen to that Jay Z song, Dotty. That's classical hip hop, complete with Hamlet references."

Vi was impressed.

Really, not-Chuck was well-read for a guy living his best life on the fringe in the Hamptons. Despite her determination to remain detached, Violet was intrigued. It was a shame that the chauffeuring cowboy came with a warning sign and wasn't to be encouraged. Even his name was wrong.

Grandma Dotty shimmied into the studio.

Violet sighed as she slid out of the car on Dotty's side. She was her grandmother's designated adult for the summer. Or at least, until Dotty grew tired of Hampton life. And Vi was afraid there were many more early mornings ahead of her.

"Your grandmother pre-paid by credit card but didn't make a return ride reservation." There was something earnest in not-Chuck's expression and Violet had no idea why. "Do you need one?"

Violet faced him. His suit was pressed. His tie perfectly knotted. She, on the other hand, wore a wrinkled tank top and hadn't brushed her hair. Wasn't that just her luck? Good-looking men always managed to show up good-looking, while she always looked like she'd just gotten out of bed. "Must I need a ride home?"

"You must. I insist." He grinned. "I'll be back in forty-five minutes."

"Fine, Shakespeare. As long as you don't stand outside the window and watch." Violet schlepped into the studio, signing up and paying for two.

～

COOP PARKED at the local coffee shop and called Dotty's request for a return ride home into his dispatcher.

"Dotty Summer? I didn't make the connection when she called in as Dot-to-the-E." His boss and landlord Paul laughed in his chain-smoker voice. "I should have recognized the address. Dotty Summer is a legend in the Hamptons. You take good care of her, Chuck."

"Summer... Summer..." Coop muttered, thinking about how Vivi didn't believe the name *Chuck* fit him. "Why does the last name Summer sound familiar?"

"If you grew up wealthy and a male around here, I'd say it was because of the Summer sisters' Kissing Test. Those Summer sisters are a suspicious lot. If one of them was dating a guy, you can bet another would come along and try to test his affection with the offer of a kiss."

Having spent many a summer as a wealthy young man in the Hamptons, something tickled the back of Coop's memories, as if he'd either heard of this before or...

Coop's cell phone rang. It didn't have his old contacts in it, so the number wasn't identified. But he knew the number on the screen by heart.

"I've got to take this other call, Paul." Coop switched lines. "Dad? Are you okay?" Coop had given Stratton his phone number several weeks back in case of emergency. This was the first time his father or anyone in the family had reached out since he'd been given the boot.

"Where are you, son?" His father's voice was stronger than it had been two months ago, but just as filled with urgency.

"I'm in the Hamptons."

"Have you found it? On second thought, you don't need to answer. That's a no." Dad's words were filled with a disappointment that stung Coop. "If you had any idea why I sent you away, you wouldn't have gone to the Hamptons." He hung up.

A rush of frustration tangled with hot impatience in Coop's veins. He pounded the steering wheel. This was like being King Arthur sent out to find the Holy Grail without knowing what the Holy Grail was.

He took a deep, calming breath. And then another.

Think, Coop.

What had his father told him that day? To find his gift? To follow the whims of fate? Or...

"Gah!" Coop gripped the steering wheel and gave it a good shake.

Maybe he should try to call Stratton and ask for advice, not that Dad's assistant would necessarily answer. Maybe he should call his mother or one of his teenage sisters, not that he wanted to put them in the middle.

At an impasse, Coop shook his head.

But he couldn't just keep working on this hamster wheel. He needed a new perspective on fathers who considered Shakespeare a guiding light.

Maybe I should ask a Shakespearean professor.

Vivi.

Now he was onto something.

Chapter Four

"*THAT-THAT DON'T KILL ME...*" GRANDMA DOTTY boogied out of the exercise studio doing the cobra and looking none the worse for wear. Even her short mohawk was still in place.

"My hip has no hop." Violet followed, limping because muscles Vi didn't even know she had were protesting. She wanted nothing more than to fall on her bed and curl into a fetal position. "I'm all for solidarity, Grandma Dotty, but I'd prefer to stick to my walking regimen from now on."

"How about a nice long horseback ride?" Shakespeare opened the rear door of the Town Car. He looked just as handsome as he had earlier, while Violet knew she looked like a damp rag. "A ride can be a form of daily exercise in place of hip hop cardio. I'd be happy to take you both."

"No, thanks," Violet said at the same time Grandma Dotty cried, "Okay, Chuck!"

Kelcie, their blond hip hop instructor, trotted out on the sidewalk. "Ladies, if you're interested in private hip hop lessons to get up to speed, I'm available for in-home visits."

Because we're so very horrible at hip hop.

Especially Grandma Dotty, who'd muscled her way to the front row and had been a step behind the entire time, sometimes whacking her neighbor with her outstretched arms. Toward the end of class, Grandma Dotty hip-checked a woman so hard, she fell to her knees and then left before Vi had a chance to apologize.

"This day keeps getting better and better." Grandma Dotty gyrated her hips in a circle. "Private lessons. I'm practically a shoe-in."

"Great. Let's put something on the schedule. I'm relatively new here and building my personal training client list." Kelcie had the kind of bubbly, innocent, infectious demeanor, at least when she wasn't yelling at a class to shake it harder. She wore a skimpy red sports bra and skimpier black shorts as if used to wearing hardly anything at all. She glanced at their chauffeur, and her entire demeanor changed from peppy, non-threatening sales-person to schmexy woman-on-the-prowl. "*Chuck.*"

One syllable. It said a lot about not-Chuck and Kelcie's history. And if Vi had to guess, that history had nothing to do with William Shakespeare.

Inexplicably, Violet was disappointed. In not-Chuck for being *that guy*. And in herself for wanting her handsome cowboy to be as dateless and single as she was.

"Kelcie. Long time, no see." Shakespeare gave off no aura that said he'd done the deed with the hip hop cardio instructor. In fact, his demeanor projected a friend-zone vibe that Vi wanted to believe. "How's that crowd performance anxiety coming along?"

"Say what?" Grandma Dotty did a double-take, nearly losing her balance since she had one foot in the air and had been on her way to a seat inside the Town Car. "You used to have stage fright, Kelcie? Me, too."

Violet contained an eye-roll. Her grandmother had never had a problem stepping into the spotlight. Or stealing it, for that matter. All in good fun, of course.

"I can confess to you, Kelcie." Grandma Dotty lowered her voice conspiratorially. "Being a runway model is on my bucket list. I'm afraid my hippity-two-step won't be good enough to model for Xuri. You know, she's sending over a coat for me to practice my runway moves with."

"O.M.G.!" Kelcie gushed, finally ripping her eyes off not-Chuck. "Is Xuri looking for hip hop dancers? I heard she was in town. I totally qualify."

"Not to mention, you've conquered your stage fright," Vi mumbled, gesturing for her grandmother to get in the car.

Not-Chuck caught her eye and mouthed, *"Behave."*

He might just as well have cautioned her not to misbehave because Vi couldn't stop looking at his lips while Dotty and Kelcie gushed over Xuri's fashions, runway shows, and cutting-edge promotional stunts.

Vi was no better than Kelcie, the cardio instructor!

"My eyes..." Not-Chuck leaned closer to Vi and wiggled his fingers in front of those brown orbs. "...are up here."

Violet's cheeks burned hotter than they had during her work out.

Shakespeare handed her a bottle of water. "You look like you need to cool off."

Vi gritted her teeth. She chugged down half the bottle and then nudged her grandmother, interrupting her conversation with Kelcie. "Time to go." Before Chuck's constant scrutiny and mischievous smile got to her and she made like a starfish and attached her limbs to his body.

"I'm sure if Xuri saw you dance, you'd be next in line," Grandma Dotty told Kelcie, inching to the car once more. She tapped a thumb to her chest. "You'd be next in line after me, of course."

"Of course! We have to talk more about this, Dotty. Say two p.m. today during our lesson?" Kelcie toggled screens on her phone. "I've got another class to teach now but you'll find my private lesson pricing quite fair."

Violet heaved a sigh. So much for keeping her grandmother's bucket list aspirations in check. Hip hop was going to be the theme of the week.

"Water, Dotty?" Shakespeare handed her grandmother a water bottle. For someone who'd practically kidnapped Vi on horseback and knew he had sex appeal to spare, he could be a nice guy. "Time to get going."

"Yes. I've got work to do," Vi added, reminding herself that Harvard professors didn't have Hampton flings. Plus, the motor was running. She could feel the cold air from the limo's air conditioning teasing her sweaty mess of a body with the promise of a refrigerator-like climate. She hopped in.

Once they were settled and on their way home, Shakespeare was back to charming them. "I was serious about that ride, ladies. No charge. I exercise horses over at the Beeswax Farm. You'd be doing me a favor."

"I've always wanted to race horses on a beach," Grandma Dotty said in a faraway voice. Her head was tipped back. Her eyes closed. She snored softly.

Violet caught not-Chuck's gaze in the rear view mirror. She pressed a finger to her lips.

"Anyway," he whispered. "Riding with you would be no problem. Single this time." He flashed her that lady-killer smile of his. "Or double if you prefer."

"Pass," Violet whispered back. "I'm not here to soak up the sun." Or indulge in flirtations with reckless strangers. "I'm writing a book on Shakespeare, and I have a deadline approaching." A looming one in August. "I've got to be diligent with my time because I imagine there are more hip hop cardio lessons in my future."

"Speaking of lessons..." Not-Chuck glanced at her in the rear view. "I'd like to talk to you about Shakespeare. Maybe a little tutoring in exchange for a horseback ride?"

"Not interested." Besides, she didn't believe he was sincere about Shakespeare. In her experience, no man she'd met outside of academia found the works of William Shakespeare to be a titillating topic of conversation.

"I have legitimate questions, Vivi, about specific quotes I'm interested in."

"Right. Like *To be or not to be?*" Violet shook her head. "Don't tease me about my life's work just to get a date."

"I'm not teasing." But not-Chuck didn't discount the date aspect of such a conversation. He turned into their driveway. "At least, listen to the quotes I want clarity on."

"You're persistent. I'll give you that." But Vi wasn't going to let him corner her. She woke Grandma Dotty and hustled her inside the house without looking back.

~

NOT one to give up easily, Coop saddled up two of Beeswax Farm's oldest horses that afternoon and headed toward the beach. He'd put English saddles on them even though he wore Western garb because Beeswax Farm was a hunting and dressage facility. But Coop was one hundred percent Texan.

He rode Boots, a black gelding with white socks, and led Yancy, a tall chestnut mare, behind him. Despite Vivi's protests, he planned to prove he was earnest when it came to Shakespeare. His future depended on it!

He would be completely serious in his request, if only there wasn't something about Vivi that called to him in a way that was both familiar and new. He enjoyed her company, as he'd done with many women in the past. But he was always able to walk away from women without a backward glance.

Until he'd met Vivi Summer.

Coop rode up the beach to the back of the Summer house. He dismounted and led both horses into the backyard. It was easy enough since there was no fence separating the property from the beach. He fastened their reins to a low-hanging tree branch in the shade. And then he took the narrow path toward the house.

And the house...

It wasn't shabby. He'd known that, having seen the front. But the back...

The main wing of the house was glass, from the first floor to the second floor. The large living room could easily hold a hundred guests, all able to enjoy the unfettered view of the ocean. On the second floor, the windows revealed what looked like a lavish master suite, including a bathroom. Very voyeuristic. The extensive wings to either side were traditionally walled and windowed.

As he neared the pool with its large rock waterfall, he spotted Dotty in the living room dancing with Kelcie.

He'd met Kelcie earlier this summer at a party, one of many he'd attended with the hardworking community that made the Hamptons a rich man's playground. While Coop had been interested in conversation, Kelcie had made it clear she wanted something more. Not just a date or a boyfriend though. Kelcie was looking to find her place in the Hamptons. She had an interest in fitness and dance and was trying to overcome some insecurities. He'd given her a pep talk and made an introduction to the owner of the fitness studio where she currently worked. He was happy things were working out for her. But he wasn't attracted to Kelcie the way he was to Vivi.

Vivi.

She sat out on the back patio beneath an umbrella, pounding away on a laptop. A skull paperweight sat atop a stack of papers. Several ancient-looking books were piled around her workspace in a semi-circle. Her long brown hair cascaded from a high, messy ponytail. She wore a pair of black-framed reading glasses, a maroon Harvard T-shirt, a pair of loose-fitting capris and blue, slip-on sneakers.

Most monied Hamptonistas clung to their fashionable existence even when relaxing in the privacy of their own home. Not his Vivi. She was down to earth.

Muffled music came from the living room, mingling with the muted sound of the ocean and a horse's snort.

Vivi didn't look up when he climbed the steps of the pool deck. But she didn't frown either, which he took as a plus.

"Hey, Vivi. It's time for a quick exchange of lessons."

"I didn't agree to that." She continued her clackity-clack on the keyboard at such a pace that he doubted she was typing anything of significance.

"Life in the Hamptons is all about trying new things and seeking life balance." You either found balance or you partied so hard you required a vacation from your vacation. Coop took a seat next to her. He swiveled the skull paperweight to face him. It was a pottery skull painted a bright orange, more of a Day of the Dead piece than a more traditional Shakespearean skull. "*Alas, poor Yorick.*"

She made a non-committal noise.

He wanted to lean closer and see if she still smelled of wild-flowers.

Instead, he asked, "What does it mean? *Alas, poor Yorick.*"

She glanced at him above those narrow readers, hands poised on the keyboard. "It's from Hamlet, as you probably know. It's a reference to the brevity of human life."

The living room door opened. Music, Dotty, and Kelcie spilled out.

"Look, Vi! We're traveling down the runway." Dotty danced her way across the pool deck, followed by Kelcie.

"Lookin' good, ladies," Coop said good-naturedly.

"You guys look great," Vivi agreed, ducking her head and typing once more.

Kelcie and Dotty circled the table where Coop and Vivi sat, and then they danced back to the living room and closed the door. The pair collapsed on the couch and laughed as if they'd had the best of times.

Coop checked the time on his cell phone. He'd be expected back soon. Rafi liked him. But Rafi wanted order in the barn and staff. "What are you working on so diligently?"

"My book." *Clack-clackity-clack-clack.* Vivi had one of those stiff keypads that made a lot of noise. "Shakespeare and the human condition. This chapter is about how people label fate a coincidence."

Her topic was perfect. "Our meeting was fate. You, me, Shakespeare."

"Now see? This is a perfect example of a coincidence. Because fate..." She tsked. "You have *player* written all over your face. I bet if you were wealthy and I googled you, you'd have a string of famous women you dated in your bio. Would those women say at first that meeting you was fate? And what would they say after you dumped them? Fate is everlasting according to Will Shakespeare, not episodic."

"Geez, Vivi. You wound me." With her accuracy. He wished he could erase his past, if only to look better to her, to *be* better for her. "I have this quote I'm interested in and—"

"A quote?" Vivi sat back, removing her reading glasses, and heaving the kind of sigh that said she didn't like interruptions. She fixed him with a firm, whiskey-colored stare. "What are you up to, Shakespeare?"

It was his turn to sigh.

He tipped his black cowboy hat back. "You're not going to talk Shakespeare to me without a good reason why, are you?"

She crossed her arms over that Harvard logo. "Nope."

"Well..." Coop glanced toward the horses, who seemed content. And then back to Vivi, who was anything but. He wasn't an open book by nature, but he was backed into a corner. "It's because of my dad."

"Oh, boy." Vivi shut her laptop, smirking. "Daddy issues."

"It's not like that." Coop frowned.

She arched her finely shaped eyebrows. He wanted to trace them with his finger.

"Okay, maybe it is like that." *Just a little.* "My dad had a heart attack and—"

"Oh, no. I'm so sorry." It was the first kind opening she'd

given him since he'd caught sight of her on the beach yesterday. And it was based on a misunderstanding. "Is he..."

"He's much better," Coop rushed on to say. "But—"

"He had lasting side-effects? Oh, man." Vivi reached over and gripped his hand.

And of its own accord, Coop's heart went pound.

Pound-pound-pound.

In a way it didn't usually beat with a woman.

And Coop liked women. He liked the way they smelled, their softness, and the complicated way they saw things. He could listen to a woman talk for an hour and know just what she needed to make her happy. His father often called his mother and his much younger sisters Drama Queens. But whatever was going on with his mom and sisters, Coop liked to hear it. He enjoyed pointing out what to him was the obvious, the way he'd pointed out to Kelcie that she was "on stage" all the time anyway. Why should standing up in front of an exercise class be any different?

But with Vivi, Coop didn't see anything he could fix.

She was clever and self-assured. She had purpose and clarity. Unlike him, her life seemed to be on track. She didn't seem to need anyone or anything.

Or worse, *want* anyone. Specifically, him. It was odd for a woman to be immune to his charm.

A pile of books tumbled between them. The books slid in the direction of the living room where Dotty could be heard laughing.

Vivi sighed, straightening the books.

And suddenly, Coop knew what Vivi needed. She needed to live life rather than sit around and watch all the time. But she'd never admit it.

"What's that quote about seizing the day?" Coop drew Vivi to her feet, surprised when she came willingly. "I've got to get these horses some exercise and then return them to a cool, shady pasture. And you're in need of exercising a different set of muscles than your sit-bones."

"Sit-bones aren't muscles." But Vivi followed him, her small hand embracing his larger one.

Coop spared her a smile. "What would Shakespeare say about you sitting all day and squinting at small print?"

She didn't hesitate to answer. "*How far that little candle throws its beams.*"

"There's one my dad used to say. What does it mean to you?"

"It means even small things have mighty impact." Vivi laughed a little as they walked past the pool. "There was a very successful college basketball coach who used to say, *"Little things make big things happen."* It's the same concept."

Coop was impressed she'd made the link. He never had, but then again, he'd never dwelled too much on Shakespearean quotes. "The coach you're talking about is John Wooden. He has the most basketball championship wins in NCAA history."

The more Vivi talked, the more Coop was convinced that she'd be able to shed light on the mysterious quest his father had sent him on.

"It wasn't that Shakespeare had all this insight on his own," Vivi said in an excited voice that matched the sudden spring to her step. "He wasn't a prophet. He was just really good at putting words and themes in his stories that captured the human experience and perspective. Words and themes that are still relevant today."

Coop nodded as they approached the horses. "Like lives are short and pay attention to detail?"

The black gelding greeted him with a nose to Coop's hat, knocking it to the ground.

"He's as annoyed with your interruption of his siesta as I am with your interruption of my work." Vivi bent to pick up his cowboy hat, dusted it off, and placed it on Coop's head.

Their gazes lingered.

Pound-pound-pound.

Not only did she make his pulse race, Vivi made him long for something he couldn't define. And it had nothing to do with

Shakespeare and everything to do with long, quiet conversations that covered everything and nothing.

"I have questions about Shakespeare." Coop handed her Yancy's reins, expecting to help her mount, but Vivi swung into the saddle on her own. "You said old Will believed in fate?"

"Yes. But remember that I don't." So glib. That was her response any time he came too close physically or verbally.

"I'm not sure why you don't take me seriously."

"Because nobody normal ever wants to talk about Shakespeare." Vivi turned Yancy around and headed down to the beach.

Coop had to hustle to mount up and follow. "Uh, sidebar. When did you learn how to ride? All that panic yesterday and—"

"Yesterday, I had nothing to hold onto—"

"Except me." He patted a spot above his belt buckle.

"—*but* you." She gave him that superior smirk of hers. "I had a well-rounded education which included all kinds of *quote-unquote* useful skills, like how to ride, how to swing a golf club, and how to hail a cab when it's snowing."

"Nobody takes cabs anymore," Coop noted. "They Uber or Lyft."

"Or order gas-guzzling, black Town Cars." She tried to hide a smile.

And he couldn't hide his. "There are lots of ways to get around, including horseback riding." He patted Boots. "Can I at least toss out my academic question?"

"If you must." But she tried to urge Yancy into a trot or gallop, giving away her unwillingness to answer.

Thankfully, Yancy was older than Mother Earth and had only one speed—slow. The mare kept plodding forward in the sand despite Vivi's attempts to the contrary.

Coop told Vivi the quote he was interested in—*like madness is the glory of this life*—explaining how his father had prefaced it by telling him to find his fate or his gift. Or both.

Vivi turned thoughtful. "The first meaning is the most obvious, that a frivolous, or glorified life, will lead to ruin. Over-spending and such. Is there a family business he might be concerned with?"

"Yes," Coop said tightly. "That's what I thought when I looked up the quote online. But it doesn't mention a gift."

"Hold that thought about the gift," Vivi said with a furrow in her brow. "You probably didn't dig deep enough to find the broader meaning of the quote. According to Shakespeare, there's a boundary between living a life to its fullest—*happily*—and living a so-called "mad" life—*one that is wasteful*. Who can judge what is right or wrong? Because what's right for one doesn't fit another. And perhaps..." She gave him a searching glance. "Never mind."

"What?" Coop mashed his cowboy hat on his head in frustration. He felt as if he was within reach of an answer and an end to his exile. "Tell me. Even if it's bad."

She wrinkled her nose, clearly reluctant to share her opinion. "I don't know you or your father or your situation."

"But you suspect..."

She glanced out to sea and then back to him. "You have a smile that reminds me of my cousin Braydon. He works in my uncle's diamond business. And although I've heard he's a good worker, my uncle always tells him to grow up."

"Ouch."

"I'm not saying you need to grow up," she hastened to say, although perhaps not with complete believability. "Honestly, I don't think Braydon needs to grow up either. He's good at what he does. But he's also enjoying being single in New York City and dates just for companionship. To my uncle, he seems to be living aimlessly."

Coop let those words settle in. His father had hung up on him when he found out Coop was in the Hamptons, a rich man's playground. Great. "You think my father wants me to find my purpose in life. My fate, so to speak."

"Yes and no." She nodded, ponytail billowing in the ocean

breeze. "Shakespeare referred to purpose as a gift. But fate... Your personal fate is often something else entirely."

Vivi explained things so well. He was grateful for her insight. But the more they talked, the more Coop was convinced that *Vivi* was his fate. If his father had sent him out to find a passion for business, he'd be disappointed. Coop had found passion for a woman. And for once, she didn't return his interest. What would Shakespeare have to say about that?

Coop suppressed a string of curse words as he realized something else. "My father wants me to find my way, but he doesn't want me to find it within the company he wants me to inherit."

Vivi brought her horse close enough to his that she could touch his arm. It was a brief touch when he wished she'd linger. "Maybe he wants you to find your way in the world without him or your family's business. You know, get experience under your belt that can benefit the company when he wants to retire."

"My own path," Coop said slowly, nodding because it made sense. *She* made sense. On too many levels. "I've been forging my own path." Even before Dad had cut him off. "I've been working for other companies for years. But he doesn't acknowledge that as more than me just biding my time, waiting for my turn at the family helm, probably because that's what I've been doing. Just a job."

"I don't want you to take this the wrong way, but perhaps your father doesn't see limo driving or stable hand as jobs worthy of your time." Vivi guided Yancy away from him, which felt odd since they were thinking along the same lines. "What kind of business does your family run? Dry cleaning? A restaurant?"

A collection of oil fields.

Coop didn't want to tell Vivi the truth for fear her opinion of him as a monied playboy would be solidified. And if there was one thing he was sure of, it was that Vivi wouldn't have time in her day for Charles Cooper Pearson the Third.

Chapter Five

"*MY GIFT. MY PURPOSE,*" NOT-CHUCK REPEATED AS IF the concept had plagued him. And yet, the cowboy's smile was gentle, as tender as the way he looked at Violet. "No one should take charge of anything without a clear goal. I get it now."

"But you still have to prove you've found your gift," she said evenly. "How do you do that? It's almost as challenging as asking someone to prove their love for you."

He nodded, continuing to look at her.

And she...

Violet continued to seesaw between attraction and duty. She had goals, which required diligent work. He was a distraction, a man she barely knew.

Violet brought Yancy to a halt. "I should get back."

"Because I make you nervous." It wasn't a question. And the way he smiled, it sizzled a path through her veins, more jolting than a shot of espresso. "What do you think will happen if I kiss you?"

"Kiss me?" she choked out. "How did the conversation turn from you finding a meaning to your life to—"

"Us testing how combustible the chemistry would be between us?" Shakespeare was daring her.

And Violet imagined he wanted her to grab hold of that dare the way she'd grabbed hold of him yesterday on their wild horse-back ride.

"Yes," she breathed before catching herself and turning Yancy back toward the Summer house. "I'm wise enough to know better than to play with fire." But that didn't stop her from wondering what kissing not-Chuck would be like.

He brought his black horse around, walking close enough to Vi that the tip of his boot nudged her stirrup. "You think I'm the kind of guy who flirts, steals a kiss, and is never heard from again?"

"Aren't you? I bet if we kissed, I'd never see you again."

His smile grew, as did his bravado. "That is a bet I can't refuse."

Vi's breath caught. It took her a moment to collect herself.

"I was talking in hypotheticals. I'm no longer the kind of woman who takes dares from handsome strangers." She urged the old chestnut mare into a faster pace. But Yancy had one speed. And unlike not-Chuck, that speed was unhurried. "I don't know you well enough to let you kiss me."

He laughed, a rich sound that had the horses swiveling their ears around to hear better. "Well, *I* know you well enough to let *you* kiss *me*."

He's ceding control to me?

"I can tell you want to drive this bus." Shakespeare grinned. "You know that I believe this is fate. But I don't think free will means you have to fight fate. Maybe it means you can decide *when* to grab onto me again."

He wasn't just her kind of sexy. He was her kind of intellectual, able to talk about things that interested her on multiple levels like the concept of fate versus free will. She wanted to kiss him. And it excited her that he wanted that kiss, too. He made her feel like Violet Summer, pre-Harvard, the woman who attended Coachella and dated men who weren't interested in settling down.

I should ignore him.

She was Professor Summer, after all.

But, oh, the power. Her body was already tingling with an overload of attraction. And to set the pace...

"I'm a college professor," she said out loud. "I'm too old for this kind of frivolity."

"But you were a rebel when you were younger." His gaze stroked over Violet, leaving a trail of heat in its wake. "I can tell. And I can tell you want to relive your youth."

She touched her cheek with the back of her hand, wondering how he knew. "There will be no kiss for the devil incarnate." For surely, that's what he was. A man sent to tempt her dedication to achieving Harvard tenure.

"Nice reference to Shakespeare's Henry the Fifth," he said, pushing her buttons all over again.

All that beauty, all that brawn, all that intellect.

It was a good thing this stretch of beach was always deserted. There were no witnesses to note the slow erosion of her defenses. She wanted to kiss him. She wanted to feel the press of his lips against hers. She wanted to grab onto that muscular body and hold on as her mind went blank and her knees went weak.

She stared straight ahead.

I shouldn't.

She was a boring associate literature professor at Harvard. Boring associate professors at Harvard had a better chance of becoming full professors. She was a Summer, of the society page Summers. And the Hamptons was a hotbed of gossip.

I won't.

And still, she gauged the distance to the Summer property line to be about one hundred yards. She calculated the odds of returning to work without kissing the cowboy as a one-to-one ratio. Even money.

Not-Chuck settled his cowboy hat more firmly on his head. "You're trying to talk yourself out of it."

"Yes." Violet couldn't look at him. Not-Chuck brought to mind moonlit swims on warm summer nights, calling in sick to work on Monday to stay home to talk, to laugh, to snuggle. "You... Kissing you would derail me."

"And yet, you still have regrets about not letting me kiss you yesterday."

Vi refused to answer him.

They approached the property line and the path to her family's house.

They approached the point where she'd say her goodbyes and walk back to stacks of Shakespeare's works and her lists of characters who'd been unable to dodge their fate.

She dismounted, sneakers landing in the soft sand. She flipped Yancy's reins over the mare's head and came around, holding them toward not-Chuck, who'd dismounted as well. "Thank you for the ride and the...the stimulating conversation."

Stimulating? Come on, Vi.

Her cheeks began to heat.

He didn't take the reins from her. "Vivi—"

"You shouldn't call me that. My name is Violet. Or Vi." Or Professor Summer. She extended the reins closer to him.

Yancy tossed her nose, bumping Violet's arm, as if to say, *"Kiss him, you fool."*

"Do you know what I've discovered about people who protest too much?" Not-Chuck's voice was low and gruff, filled with the same yearning Vi was fighting. "They're just arguing with themselves. You want to kiss me, Vivi. *Alas, poor Yorick.* Life is too short not to reach out for what you want. That is, reach for what you want badly."

Violet had had enough of his arguments and her excuses. She grabbed hold of those pearly snaps covering that muscular chest, yanked him forward, and kissed him with all the abandon of the woman she used to be.

∾

VIVI IS DEFINITELY no delicate flower.

And for that, Coop was grateful.

Vivi's kiss was all-in. This was no tentative approach. No polite brush of lips. She kissed him the way a woman did when she'd been wondering about the experience and couldn't walk away without knowing—

She stepped back, panting a little, sweet face aflame with color.

—what their kiss would be like.

A smile built on Coop's face, the kind that etched itself into cheeks and memories. He wanted her to kiss him again. Longer. Slower.

"I'll be going now," Vivi said, gaze traveling everywhere but across his face.

She didn't move.

"You'll think about that kiss later," Coop said softly, teasingly. There was something brewing between them, like a summer storm over the Hamptons when the wind stalled. Attraction was thick in the air between them, keeping them standing within touching—*kissing*—distance. And he, for one, knew exactly what he wanted to do about it—kiss Vivi again! "I'll call you later."

Her shocked gaze landed on his face. "You don't have my number."

Oh, he had her number, all right. She was a woman who paid too much attention to appearances. But she was ready for romance and the right man to keep her on her toes, the way she'd keep her man on his.

"The name Vivi suits you. Violet is the business-like professor. Vi is the caring granddaughter. But Vivi..." Coop resisted reaching for a lock of her thick, wayward hair. "Vivi trusts the tide to take her somewhere new and exciting. Vivi isn't scared to climb into a sailboat without a destination. Vivi doesn't wait for the man she's interested in to set the pace. She's in charge of the play, just like Shakespeare."

Her jaw dropped open, but she said nothing.

Coop pried Yancy's reins from her tensely-curled fingers, tipped his hat, and swung up in the saddle.

He rode off, not exactly into the sunset. But he could feel Vivi's gaze upon him and he didn't look back.

~

"Look at my Xuri jacket, Vi." Grandma Dotty was waiting for Violet in the living room when she returned from her little ride with Chuck.

She could no longer refer to him as *not-Chuck*. Not after that wowzer of a kiss.

No. He was Chuck, who was interested in and familiar with Shakespeare. He was Chuck, who made her wish she'd met him a year from now after she'd achieved tenure. He was Chuck, who kissed exactly as that mischievous smile promised.

And speaking of promises, he'd promised to call her. Now, Violet would look at every unfamiliar number that showed up on her cell phone screen and wonder if it was him or a pre-recorded message reminding her that her car warranty had lapsed and needed renewing. Not that she owned a car anymore, but those spammers couldn't even target car owners. They called her all the time.

"Ain't I bombin', Vi?" Grandma Dotty wore a black one piece bathing suit underneath an oversized white denim, puffy jacket with cute blue bunnies painted on the back and blue-gray faux fur trimming the sleeves and hood. The jacket hem hung down to her knobby knees. Overall, the coat was so large, it could have fit two Grandma Dotties inside.

"You are *da* bomb," Violet confirmed, flopping onto the couch and staring at her table out by the pool where her work awaited. And would wait. Racing memories of charming cowboys weren't going to allow her to concentrate just yet. Somewhere, music was playing, but Vi's jumbled thoughts wouldn't let her identify the song. She was adrift in the feeling of being held by strong arms and kissed like she was Chuck's brand of hotness.

Dr. Violet Summer wasn't hot. She was a well-respected, up-and-coming professor.

And yet...

She covered her face with her hands and groaned.

"Vi! Are you listening to me?" Her grandmother backed into Violet's line of sight, trying to do the running man. "And one. And two. And three. And four." Her cheeks were bright red and sweat had finally defeated her short mohawk.

"The coat is awesome." But looked out of place on her grandmother. And something else was out of place. "Why are you dancing to the soundtrack from *West Side Story*?" The music came from the stereo across the room.

"That hip hop music was giving me a headache." Grandma Dotty sank on the sofa, practically disappearing inside her jacket with the hood flipped up. "Did I miss our horseback ride?"

"Yes. Chuck has come and gone." Like Kelcie, cardio and dance instructor, who was nowhere to be seen. And speaking of the bubbly blonde, "We aren't going to hip hop cardio in the morning, are we?"

"No." Grandma Dotty slouched deeper in her seat with a disappointed sigh. "Kelcie only teaches hip hop cardio on Mondays and Fridays. She invited us to marching camp tomorrow morning though."

Marching camp? Did I miss the latest exercise craze?

There had to be an explanation. "Um... You mean band camp? Does Kelcie think you can learn something from a band majorette?" And more importantly, was this something Vi could skip?

"No." Her grandmother peered from beneath a fluff of blue-gray faux fur. "Kelcie said we'd be racking up the vegetables."

Marching bands? Vegetables? Add that to the residual impact of hot kisses. Vi was too confused to speak.

"Ending in a squash party," Grandma Dotty said as if she knew what she was talking about. "I pre-paid our attendance because it sounded like so much fun. Really, Vi. Get with the times. Marching camp is all the rage."

"Oh." Understanding dawned and not happily. "You signed us up for *boot camp* with a *squat party*?"

"Yes, yes. That's it." Grandma Dotty sat up, hood falling away and jacket falling from her skinny shoulders until she looked like she was emerging from a puffy white sleeping bag. "Kelcie said I'd dance better for Xuri if we did her marches."

Vi groaned. "Must I go?"

"Yes. Do you know what keeps me young and mentally sharp?" Grandma Dotty stood, gathering her jacket in her arms. She gave Vi a haughty stare. "New things. It's why I have a bucket list. Now, don't argue. I've already called for a ride in the morning and requested Chuck as our driver."

Violet groaned again, grabbing a nearby pillow, and crushing it to her face.

～

COOP KNEW he had nothing to smile about.

He had nothing his father wanted—no gift, no life goal, no meaningful existence planned, other than getting Vivi to kiss him again.

He smiled anyway. He smiled through exercising a variety of horses in the arena at Beeswax Farm. He smiled through helping Rafi finish mucking out stalls. He smiled during the drive into town in his barely held-together pickup and back to the small apartment he shared with his boss Paul over Lotus Imports & Motor Repair.

Coop parked in the back lot next to an older model Ferrari with its hood up and a Corvette with a flat tire.

Paul walked out of the garage, phone in one hand, container of engine oil in another. "Yes, Mrs. Greenburg. We'll have a driver to you promptly at seven." He hung up and handed Coop his phone, wiping a bead of sweat dotting his gray hairline. "Put those details in the car service calendar for me, will you?"

"Sure." Coop entered the information in Paul's app. And then he checked the schedule for the early morning shift. "Dotty Summer's going to exercise early again." He shamelessly entered Dotty's phone number into his own phone. The sweet old gal liked him. She'd divulge Vivi's number.

"You know my kid is coming out next week, right?" Paul had finished putting oil in the classic Ferrari. He closed the hood. "I hate to do this to you, Chuck, but I need that bed you're sleeping on a week from Friday."

Coop's smile wavered. Everyone in the Hamptons who wasn't wealthy seemed to struggle with affordable housing. Coop had known his time renting from Paul was coming to an end, but he'd hoped for a few more weeks. "I'll find something." Not his family's house. His father would never approve of that. But someone had to have a spare bed somewhere.

"I'll ask around, too, kid."

The two men walked toward the garage.

"I'm going to grab a sandwich at the deli." And then Coop needed a shower and to change into his suit to drive wealthy vacationers who wanted to avoid the hassle of parking to-and-from dinner. "Want anything?"

"No, thanks. Delilah invited me to dinner." Paul chuckled. "She's a good cook and her engine needs a tune-up again."

"You two say you're bartering, but I think Delilah is sweet on you."

"Wouldn't matter." Paul tsked. "When I got divorced, I vowed never to dance another round with love."

The two men parted ways.

Coop walked out of the back lot, passing the main office and its lavish waiting room, bringing Dotty's number up on his phone and preparing to give her a call.

The door to the office swung open behind him. "Coop? Cooper Pearson?"

No one in town knew his real name. Closing his phone screen without calling, Coop turned slowly, recognizing the man immediately. Bright blond hair, tall, lean frame, and a polished smile. "Simon! Great to see you." In a way, it was. Simon was part of Coop's old life.

"I didn't know you were vacationing in the Hamptons." Simon hurried forward and shook Coop's hand with a firm grip. He was from a Houston family who'd made their fortune in I.T. designing software exclusively for Fortune 500 companies. Their families traveled in the same circles. "My Ferrari had an oil leak. That's what I get for driving an old classic."

"That sucks." Coop chuckled politely, commiserating. "What are you doing here? I thought you were in New York." After dropping out of college several years ago, he'd gone to culinary school. And last year, he'd been on one of those cooking competition shows on TV.

"I've been searching for my place in the world, I suppose." Simon paused, looking as if he couldn't believe he'd admitted such a thing. "Trying to raise funding for a restaurant, if you must know."

Coop felt a sudden kinship for a fellow silver-spooner now making his way alone in the world. "Good luck with that."

"Thanks." Simon visibly relaxed. "I've got a part-time gig as a sous chef at The Palm. I'm also giving private cooking lessons and working for a catering company."

"Working hard for the money," Coop muttered. He knew how that went.

"Looks like you broke down in the middle of a horseback ride." Simon pointed at Coop's dirty western wear. "I didn't know your family kept horses up here."

"Well, everything changes, I suppose," Coop said vaguely, not wanting to admit his situation outright. He made a show of pulling out his cell phone and checking the time. "I've got to go. But maybe I'll see you around."

"Lots of parties this weekend." Simon nodded. "Fair warning. I might be working at a couple."

"I have a lot more respect for hard workers than you might think." Coop meant it.

"Mr. Marchand?" Delilah poked her head out of the waiting room door. Her unnaturally red hair glinted in the sunlight. "Your car is fixed. Paul's bringing it around."

"Great." Simon walked backward toward the office. "Nice seeing you, Coop."

Coop waved, resuming his walk toward the deli but at a slower pace.

It felt like his old life was catching up to him.

And just when he was starting to like his new one.

～

IT WAS HALF-PAST nine at night when Violet's cell phone rang.

She was in bed, jotting down some handwritten notes about fate from a collection of Shakespeare's comedies. Many of his characters fought the fate society dictated to disastrous results.

Our meeting was fate.

That was Chuck speaking, his words floating around in her head.

Vi groaned, not wanting to think about her Hamptons cowboy, passionate kisses, or the possibility that fate had brought her the man of her dreams. She may respect Shakespeare's insight into human nature, but she did not share his belief about fate.

The phone chimed again, a gentle counterpoint to Grandma Dotty's soft, consistent snores down the hall.

Violet set down her rag-eared notebook, staring at the phone display. "I don't recognize you."

That didn't stop the phone from continuing to chime.

Violet peered at the number. "It's a gamble as to whether this is my kissing cowboy or just a recorded message telling me I qualify for satellite TV service."

She pressed the green answer button anyway and raised the phone to her ear. But she said nothing, just in case it was a spammer.

"Vivi?"

"Shakespeare." She still preferred that name to Chuck. "How did you get my number?"

"I've missed you, too." His voice was deep and smooth, tinged with the same excitement she was feeling.

It was a bit alarming how just hearing his voice made her feel happy. She reached for her snark arsenal. "I bet your schtick works on all the girls."

"I don't care about all the girls. Just one."

Oh, my-oh, my-oh, my.

Her pulse quickened. How she wanted the feelings blossoming inside of her to be real and for him to be the kind of man the Harvard tenure review committee wouldn't look down upon. How could they find fault in a hardworking, blue collar man? If only he didn't exude the kind of confidence she'd come to expect from wealthy, successful men who craved the spotlight. "Are you calling to let me know you found your gift?" His purpose in life.

"Not exactly." Was that regret in his voice? It must hurt to be cast out by his father the way he'd been. "I've spent the past few hours thinking about how I could make you smile more. Flowers seem too cliché. Candlelight dinners seem too boring. And—"

"I meant, did you find a purpose your father would approve of?" Because she was certain his father wouldn't accept Chuck back into the fold with a life goal of making Violet smile more. And she wanted Chuck to be happy.

Isn't that what couples want for each other? Happiness?

Violet bit her lip and cautioned herself to slow down. Way, way down.

"I like to work," Chuck deadpanned.

"You say that as if it's a surprise to you. Everybody works."

"I like to work with horses," he said quickly. "And if I could get paid for it, I like to talk to you about Shakespeare."

"Such a flatterer." She enjoyed talking to him about the old bard, too.

"Yes, that's me. Yancy was swayed by my praise earlier." His voice was rich and tempting. "The mare nibbled at my ear after our ride. The flirt."

The flirt...

The words struck Violet sharply, resounding with danger instead of romantic tease. "Are you ever serious?" Could he ever be?

The line went silent for more than a little while and Vi hated it. She hated that she couldn't just enjoy a light flirtation for what it was. She stared at the framed picture hanging near her bedroom door—a field of yellow sunflowers raised to the afternoon sun.

She felt like those sunflowers when he was around, lifting her face to bask in the warmth of his attention.

Chuck sighed heavily. "I thought I was serious today, when we talked about my father."

"I'm sorry. You're right." *Please don't hang up.*

And also, please don't hurt me.

But Vi knew the only way to protect herself was to put up her guard.

"I take it you don't like it when I make you smile, Vivi."

Oh, she liked it. She liked it too much. "Shakespeare..."

"I like it when you call me Shakespeare." Some of the playfulness returned to his tone.

It was her turn to smile. And yet... "*Shakespeare...*" It had to be said. "This can't happen, not long-term."

"Because we're from two different worlds?" There was an edge to his question.

"No. Because my life is in Boston and my time is taken up by my work." That was a convenient excuse. "I have one shot at tenure at Harvard. The next few months are critical for me. And along you come with your steamy looks..."

You could ruin everything.

"You're driven and settled," he said slowly. "And maybe that's what I like about you. Other women look at me as if I'm a specialty chocolate they want to hoard. You look at me as if I'm a man you can't figure out but want to."

She laughed, glad to return to safer waters. "That much is true."

"But Vivi," his voice softened, lowered. And more than anything, she wanted to see the warmth in his eyes when he spoke. "If there's more to me for you to discover and more of you for me to discover, don't you want to explore the unknown? Together?"

I do.

But also, I don't.

Now was the time to re-iterate that they had no future together. Quickly, like the fast removal of a sticky bandage.

"I was hired at Harvard in May, but I didn't start until September. I'd just completed my Ph.D. and I needed to let off some steam." Although her family knew, Violet didn't tell strangers this story. Ever. But there was something about Chuck that inspired her trust. "I went to a party with my sister Kitty, and I met someone..."

"Careful now," Chuck said in a husky voice. "I'm suddenly realizing I have a jealous streak. At least, when it comes to you."

Vi would have laughed if her message wasn't serious. "He was a NASCAR driver and without realizing it, I got caught up in something... Well, that sounds wrong. Let's say that he was successful, very photogenic and suddenly, I was a minor celebrity." That was probably a stretch. "Or at least, I was in Harvard's eyes. I showed up for my onboarding and was told—not in this specific language—that Harvard professors represent Harvard in responsible way. I understood it to mean rich, jet-setting, party girls have no place teaching at Harvard."

"Did you like this guy? The NASCAR racer?"

"That's none of your business." There was no way Vi was admitting just how much her heart had been broken six years ago. "I will tell you that he passed my sisters' Kissing Test, but in the end, I had to choose between him and my dreams." That sounded like a badly written romcom with a disappointing ending. She tried to lighten things. "You know, I fit the Harvard mold now. I wear flannel pajamas and sweat socks at home after work. And I bring books to bed with me."

"That sounds super sexy, Vivi." He sighed. "But I'm sorry you had to choose."

"Me, too," Vi said softly, although looking back, the hurt didn't sting near as much now as it had before. She wanted to say it was a good thing he was just an everyday Joe, but that would re-open the door to a relationship. And the whole purpose of sharing her past was to make clear that the attraction between them had no future.

Chuck cleared his throat. "Tell me more about this Kissing Test. Someone else mentioned it to me today. Apparently, the Summer Kissing Test is legend in these parts. And if winning your trust means passing this trial, I need a briefing."

"That would imply the test lies ahead of you." She smiled. How did he keep doing that? "But for educational purposes. It's not a legend. You might find this hard to believe, but some men are more interested in the fortune a woman will someday inherit than the woman herself."

"*No.*" He sounded aghast.

"It's true," she reassured him, enjoying their banter. "And so, my oldest sister Kitty came up with the Kissing Test. I have four sisters, each beautiful in their own way. And if a man wants to be in a relationship with me and earn my family's approval, he has to be immune to the charm of my sisters and their attempted kisses."

"I... How long has this test been going on?" He sounded distracted.

"Over a decade, I think." Violet was struck by a sudden suspicion. "Did you grow up in the Hamptons?" Because there had been many a summer spent at the shore, in town, at parties. Executing Kissing Test campaigns.

"Vivi, I'm not a local. I'm a Texan." He sounded offended.

Still, there was the uncertainty with which he'd asked that question about when the tests had begun.

"I have to go," Chuck said over the sound of voices and a car starting in the background. "Sweet dreams of me, Vivi." And then he hung up without giving her a chance to tell him she would do nothing of the sort.

It was a good thing she didn't.

Because she dreamed of him all night.

∾

COOP DROVE the Greenburgs to a gelato store, let them out, and then pulled around the corner to await their call for a pick-up.

The gelato store...

It was a classy place with French décor. A decade ago, it had more of a fast food vibe with wooden picnic tables, outdoor speakers playing Top 40 hits, and prices that didn't gouge. It had been a hot spot for college kids in the summer, serving gelato and espresso.

Coop had hung out there often. That's where he learned about the weekend's parties, talked to girls, and maybe stole a kiss or two.

Vivi had said her sister started their Kissing Test a decade earlier, give or take. That would fit the timeline of summer nights at the gelato store, a kind of ominous timeline, at least the more he thought about it. Because Coop vaguely remembered kissing a brunette. Her name might have been Kitty or Kathy. And the next night at the gelato store, he'd been approached by her sister and lip-bombed. He couldn't remember the sister's name. But she'd had thick, long hair and had kissed thoughts of Kitty or Kathy right out of his head.

What if the second sister was Vivi? What if that's why he found her irresistible today? Was this fate at work?

Coop washed a hand over his face.

Maybe it was best to let old memories stay in the past.

So much of his life was up in the air. He had to hold on tight to the good things today.

Like Vivi.

Chapter Six

"Nobody told me boot camp was thirty minutes earlier than hip hop cardio," Vivi muttered as she came slowly down the front steps the next morning, bleary-eyed and with her hair in a familiar, messy ponytail.

Coop smiled at her, handing over a small paper cup with a double shot of espresso and taking time to compare her face to that of the girl he'd kissed all those years ago. He couldn't see more than a shadow of similarity.

Truth be told, he'd been a little worried last night thinking about what Vivi had told him of the choice she'd made between love and her career. His family was prominent in Texas. And there was the article that had come out last holiday season about Coop being one of the most eligible and elusive bachelors in the southern states. He wanted to be a man Vivi could be proud of, someone who wouldn't be cause for her to lose out on tenure.

"I'm looking forward to the squash party," Dotty said, dancing her way into the car.

After a late night of driving vacationers, Coop envied the old girl her energy.

"Not squash. *Squat.* It's a *squat* party." Vivi threw back the two shots of caffeine he'd provided like it was a tequila shot. She left the empty cup on the bottom step of the front porch. "No one looks forward to squat parties, least of all me. Thanks for the espresso, Shakespeare."

"My pleasure." He held the door open for her to get in. "Did you sleep well last night?"

"Don't push your luck," she muttered, narrowing her eyes.

"I slept like a log," Dotty piped up from the back seat. "Exercise will do that for you, along with an empty house."

"Do you know what else happens in an empty house?" Vivi muttered, dropping into the seat next to her grandmother. "Sound. Any little sound. It travels through an empty house like the roar of saws working through thick logs."

"Are you saying I snore?" Dotty lost some of her perpetual good humor, enough so that Coop leaned in the open door in case he needed to referee.

"You? Snore? Grandma Dotty, no one ever says you snore." Vivi pushed Coop out and pulled her door shut but not before flashing a sarcastic expression his way.

Oh, Dotty snores, all right.

Coop hurried around the car and got in, not wanting to miss any of their conversation.

"I popped right up when my alarm went off," Dotty was saying. "I'm fresh as a daisy."

"Let's see how you feel after this squash party." Vivi leaned her head against the window and sighed.

"I take it someone isn't a morning person," Coop ventured, putting the car into gear.

"As a professor, I keep banker hours." Vivi shoved on a pair of dark glasses. "And I walk for exercise while listening to podcasts. I don't usually get up at the crack of dawn or exercise with music blaring and someone shouting at me to shake it to the left."

"New experiences keep you young," Dotty sing-songed as if she'd told Vivi this before.

Coop drove them to the small park where Kelcie held her boot camps. "I don't suppose Shakespeare's quote about wearing your heart on your sleeve could pertain to bad moods."

"It pertains." Vivi didn't look as if the idea made her happy though.

"I believe that cowboy of yours read Othello." Dotty caught Coop's eye in the rear view mirror and grinned. "No man's ever read Shakespeare for you, Vi."

"He didn't read it. His father has a habit of dropping quotes."

"I read it in high school." And again in college. Not that the deeper meanings had stuck with him.

Vivi scrubbed her forehead. "Apologies to everyone in the car. Apparently, no one should talk to me or listen to me before seven a.m. and a full cup of coffee."

"Your espresso should kick in soon," Coop said kindly as he pulled up to the curb. "And moving your body should loosen up any sore muscles from yesterday."

He would have said more, but the ladies at the park looked like Iron Man athletes, women who were attending Kelcie's squat party for some serious muscle pain. He didn't think his humor would play well against that backdrop.

In about an hour, Vivi was going to be in a world of hurt.

Dotty gleefully scrambled out and joined the rest, busting a move that really had no definition but said a lot about her *joie de vivre*.

"I keep telling myself it's my turn." Vivi got out more slowly and only when Coop had opened her door.

"You're turn for what?"

"Watching my grandmother." She rolled her shoulders back, and put her game face on, looking like a referee about to officiate a contentious Superbowl. "We grandchildren all take turns. I thought it'd be easy. I thought I'd be sitting by the pool working on my book all day while she watched talk shows."

"Dotty isn't the talk show type." Even Coop knew that.

"She's not. She's the bucket list type." Vivi walked off, carrying her water bottle and purse and a resigned expression.

"Have fun at boot camp." Despite her low spirits, Coop couldn't resist the tease.

Vivi turned and gave him a look over the top of her sunglasses that said he'd pay for that later.

Coop smiled.

I look forward to it.

❧

VIOLET WAS PAYING for all that exercise.

She had the zombie walk mastered—stiff legs, stiff arms, head tilted at an odd angle because of her stiff neck. And she had the zombie way of talking mastered, too—grunting and groaning as she went up-and-down the stairs and in-and-out of chairs.

Tuesday afternoon, Vi took a hot bath, a couple over-the-counter pain pills, and a long nap. Boot camp had done her in. But not Grandma Dotty. She had another hip hop lesson with Kelcie and was already downstairs practicing her moves.

A phone call woke Vi up around four.

"Grandma Dotty says you're dying." Maggie laughed over the sound of road noise. As a large animal vet, she spent most of the day driving to visit patients. "I told her it would take more than a couple exercise classes to do you in."

"You're wrong." Violet sat up with a grimace. "I'm done in. I don't understand how Grandma Dotty does it."

"Don't you remember? She spent time with Cousin Chad a few weeks ago. He's trying to get healthier. And she jumped in to his regimen—walking breaks throughout the day and healthier eating."

"Ah, yes." Violet remembered now. "But still, I shouldn't be out for the count. I exercise. I walk." Once a day. Sometimes. "And I'm more than half her age."

"You walk at a leisurely pace, and you don't count your steps, Vi. *Use your turn signal, you idiot!*" Maggie honked her horn —*beep, beep, beep!* "I hate Hamptons traffic in the summer."

"It's why I don't regret being here without a car." Violet took a deep breath and then staggered to her feet. "I smell cooking. Grandma Dotty's probably burning the house down." Her grandmother got distracted when she was in the kitchen, and things tended to catch fire. "I need to go." She promised to call Maggie if she needed anything and made her way slowly down the stairs to the kitchen where she heard voices and smelled delicious aromas.

"I'm going to lower the heat, Dotty." A man in chef whites with sleeves rolled up stood next to her grandmother at the stove. He was blond, with a strong profile and toned forearms. There was an undertone of strained patience in his voice. "Remember what I told you about eggs. They like to be treated gently. Best go slow, the way a woman likes to be treated."

"I've always preferred a man to go fast." Grandma Dotty scoffed and shook a wok pan over a gas burner. "You should change your metaphors, Simon. Not all women like to take it slow, and I will not judge those who don't."

"Hey. What's going on?" Violet tried to straighten her body and smooth her slow gait because Chef Simon was hot.

Not as hot as my cowboy chauffeur, but still...

Vi shook her head a little, refusing to think of Chuck when Simon smiled a greeting as she sat on a bar stool.

"Carmen in boot camp told me about cooking lessons with Chef Simon." Grandma Dotty left the stove and leaned on the island across from Violet.

Which was apparently not good, because her instructor leaped into her place at the stove and continued to shake the wok pan and stir its contents.

Her grandmother smiled happily, oblivious to the culinary danger being averted behind her. "And lucky for us, he had a last minute cancelation. I've always wanted to take cooking lessons."

"Because you hate to cook?" Violet fought a smile. "Or because you aren't a good cook?"

"Oh, the pot is calling the kettle black now." Grandma Dotty's smile didn't dim as she pantomimed a message to Violet that translated to something like, *"I brought you a hot chef. Get over to the stove and feel the heat."*

Violet shook her head. "My pots are just fine in the kitchen."

Grandma Dotty tsked, jerking her head over her shoulder in Chef Simon's direction, over and over. "As I recall, you have trouble boiling eggs, Vi." Head jerk. Head jerk. Head jerk. Translation: *Get over there by that attractive, single man.*

"Everybody has trouble boiling eggs." Violet gripped the bar stool handles, continuing the silent conversation. *I'm not going to make a play for a hot chef by pretending I can't cook.*

"I have a class for that. Boiling eggs, I mean," Chef Simon said smoothly without turning around. He had a nice, broad back.

Not as broad as Chuck's. And his hair was beginning to thin on top.

Violet frowned. "I don't care about any of that."

"Eggs?" Grandma Dotty blinked in confusion, glancing over her shoulder. "Or..."

"No...Yes...I'm sorry," Vi babbled. "What are we talking about? I'm still half asleep."

"Are you feeling all right?" The handsome chef turned to look at her with clear blue eyes that held no hidden secrets, mischief, or sorrow. "I can make soup."

"No soup!" Vi said too quickly, not wanting to encourage a man who hadn't quoted Shakespeare once.

Gah! What is happening to me?

"My grandmother is an early riser and doesn't like to let this night owl sleep. Plus, she dragged me to exercise classes two days in a row at dawn and because I'm competitive, I went all-in on hip thrusts and squat parties and..." She'd babbled her way into a corner. "This is supposed to be my summer break?" She grimaced because she never ended a sentence with a question when there should have been a period.

"Ah." Chef Simon's smile was comforting.

Not mischievous. Not pulse pounding.

In other words, not Chuck's.

Grandma Dotty mouthed, *"You like him."*

Violet shook her head. "I like *food*." Especially food she didn't cook that smelled like it came from a five-star restaurant.

The chef chuckled. Not smoothly. It was more like a barely contained donkey bray. And that sound... That cadence...

Violet looked at him with a new set of eyes. "Have we met before?"

"You've seen him." Grandma Dotty was thrilled with her catch of the day. She danced around the kitchen island and gave Violet's shoulders a squeeze. "He was on that cooking show we watch."

"*Iron Pan Warriors?*" Those chefs were awesome. "Which season?"

"Season Ten." Some of the good cheer slipped from his tone. "I didn't win."

"You lost on bay bugs." It was all coming back to Violet now. He'd lost just last year.

"Bugs?" Dotty's arms fell to her sides. "I don't remember anyone cooking bugs on that show."

"Bay bugs are like lobster but from Australia, remember?" Vi studied Chef Simon. "What are you doing here? I would have thought you'd have a restaurant open somewhere by now."

"That's my goal. I just need seed money for the right location." The confidence was returning to Simon's voice and demeanor, but now he was sounding like a pitch-man reciting his rehearsed speech. "As a chef, you've got to be selective when it comes to location, plus find an area where the local food supply chain plays to your strengths."

"I'm thinking of investing," Grandma Dotty said brightly. "Because we don't have bay bugs here."

Chef Simon gave Grandma Dotty a glowing smile, as equally bright as it was hopeful.

Violet hated to be the one to dash his hopes. "She can't invest without my father's approval."

Simon's smile fell and he returned his attention to the skillet.

"You could invest, Vi." Grandma Dotty nudged her, wobbling her white brows suggestively. "Wouldn't it be fun to have a table reserved for us at a restaurant we...*you* own?"

Violet didn't like the way Chef Simon looked at her, with interest that had nothing to do with her as a woman. He was a Kissing Test candidate for sure, appreciative of an heiress for inheritance's sake.

It was a head-snapping jolt back to reality after a few short days of Chuck's worshipful glances that she felt had nothing to do with her future net worth and everything to do with who she was today.

"I'm not liquid enough to invest. Sorry." Simon saw her for what she truly was—a dry literature professor who might have funds to invest. It made Chuck's interest in her that much harder to walk away from.

What am I going to do?

~

"It's you."

Coop turned at the feminine voice, holding the bag of apples he'd just filled.

The woman who'd called out to him stood in stained blue jeans, a wrinkled medical scrub shirt, and big black army boots. Her jet black hair floated in a tousled cloud about her head.

For the life of him, he couldn't place her.

"You're the cowboy who galloped off with my sister on a white horse." She glanced down at herself. "I was wearing my party clothes then." She glanced back up at him. "I'm Maggie. Dr.

Maggie Summer, veterinarian. I just delivered a foal and am in need of a shower, but Vi called me with an S.O.S."

Suddenly concerned, Coop closed the distance between them. "Is it Dotty? Is she in trouble?"

Maggie gave him a wry smile. "No. It's Vi. She's up late wrestling with her Shakespeare and had a craving for yogurt." She gestured toward the yogurt machine in the deli. "I agreed to bring her some since I was out this way, and it was so late." She moved toward the machine.

And he moved with her. "Vivi should rent a car while she's out here. I can't always drive her." He'd just driven some late-night diners home and ended his shift.

"*Vivi?*" Maggie took a small plastic bowl from the stack next to the machine. "I bet that gets under Professor Summer's skin."

He didn't think so, not when she kissed him the way she did.

"I see there's something brewing between you." Maggie operated the soft serve machine with practiced ease, swirling the combination of banana and chocolate into a neat presentation. She covered it with a plastic lid and set it to the side, grabbing a second bowl. "My sister isn't your type." She gave him a sideways glance. "But maybe I am."

Warning bells went off in Coop's head. He took a step back and held up a hand. "I'm not interested in you. Or your sisterly tests." The kissing kind.

Maggie gave a little laugh, glancing down at her attire. "I'm not exactly dressed for seduction, am I?"

"That wouldn't matter. You're not Vivi."

"*Vivi...*" She filled another plastic bowl with equal precision. "This can't end well for you. Vi is only here until the end of summer. Her life is in Boston."

And mine is in Texas.

But... "She needs me."

Maggie paused mid-reach for another lid. She gave him a searching glance.

"She's living too much in her head, deep-diving into Shakespeare and staying down for too long. If you study history, the greats at anything were great because they experienced life. And they brought those experiences to their work." It was an earnest speech, but he believed it.

Maggie arched her brows, much the same way Vivi had done when he'd made a similar argument.

He pressed on. "Benjamin Franklin, Albert Einstein, Leonardo da Vinci, Michelangelo. They brought a curiosity for life to their work." It had been one of the most interesting highlights of his private school education. The great minds and talents in history weren't workaholics like his father. "When you look at me, I know you see someone with two jobs and no future. I probably didn't help that impression when I rode off with your sister. And you might be right. I need to find my own path. But so does Vivi. She's stuck in one lane right now, unable to see the off-ramp because that university she works for has scared her to be something she's not."

"That's accurate, although she'd deny it." Maggie sealed the second yogurt. "Sometimes I feel the same way. Trapped, that is. I want my own practice but can't afford all the equipment on my own. And Vi..."

"She thinks she'll be happy once she has tenure." Coop clutched his bag of fruit and waited for what he hoped would be Maggie's blessing and not a lunge for his lips.

She put the two yogurts into a cardboard tray, shaking her head. "I'm not saying I'm in your corner. But I don't disagree with you about Vi either." Maggie handed the tray to Coop. "She said she'd be waiting at the pool. What was your name again?"

He took the yogurts slowly, processing that a moonlight visit with Vivi was being presented to him and trying to keep his real name from crossing his lips.

"You can call me Shakespeare." He smiled at Maggie's startled look. "It's what your sister calls me."

～

"Did someone order yogurt?"

Violet recognized that deep voice coming from the side yard. It wasn't Maggie making a delivery.

She closed her laptop and turned, making out Chuck's outline as he emerged from the shadows wearing that cheap suit that fit him so well. "Don't tell me you have my sister's phone number, too."

"Nope. We bumped into each other in the yogurt aisle. She looked beat and I'd just finished a shift so..." He sat down at the table next to Vi, close enough to make her heart start pounding faster. "Since you don't take enough personal time, I thought I'd bear witness to this yogurt craving of yours." He removed a lid and handed her a yogurt and plastic spoon. "I like you when you're in intellectual mode. But I also like you when you take time to chill."

"Did my sister try to..."

"Kiss me?" Chuck grinned. "Yeah."

Jealousy clogged Vi's throat. *She* wanted to be the only Summer sister he kissed. "And..."

"I passed on the opportunity." Oh, there was mischief in his eyes as his gaze glanced off her lips. "But so did that loser who broke your heart. I thought I'd put that out there before you did."

Violet sat back in her chair and took a spoonful of yogurt. It was refreshingly chilled, like most of her conversations with Chuck.

"How goes fate versus free will in the book?" He angled his body toward her, filling his spoon with yogurt.

"It's a slow chapter." Oh, he pretended to concentrate on eating, but she could feel his attention upon her. And she liked it! She'd like it better if he closed the distance between them and kissed her.

He chuckled, and instead of Simon's startling sound, Chuck's laughter soothed her. "You're stuck writing that section about fate for a reason. It's because we—"

"Oh, no you don't." She shook her spoon at him. "I told you.

I don't believe in fate. And it has nothing to do with this chapter. It's challenging, that's all."

Chuck shrugged, running his spoon around the rim of the yogurt cup. "If you say so."

"*If I say so,*" Violet muttered before taking a big bite of yogurt.

"Let's not argue. You'll believe in me and fate someday." He stood, staring down on her warmly. "Come on. I've had a long day and I want to put my feet in the pool." He moved to the pool without waiting for her, setting his yogurt aside while he removed his shiny black shoes and thin black socks. He rolled up his pants legs and dipped his feet in the water. "Ahh. So good."

Violet joined him, bringing her unfinished yogurt. How could she not follow him? She was as drawn to Chuck as she was to a dessert buffet. "You have proof of this fate of ours?"

"Yes." He kicked his feet slowly in the water.

"And..."

He gave her a brief, considering look. "Today isn't the day to prove it to you."

"That's a cop out." She ate more yogurt.

"You know, I'm not tied down to living in the Hamptons. I suppose where I land next will depend upon what I decide to do with the rest of my life." A furrow passed over his brow. Here and then just as quickly gone. "I could go back to Texas... Or discover if there's anything for me in Boston."

Vi finished her yogurt and set her cup to the side. His talk of moving was opening that door to a relationship again. And for some reason, she was reluctant to close it. "Have you discovered something you're passionate about? Work-wise, I mean."

"No." He moved his cup a few feet away and turned to face her. "Vivi..."

She kissed him. How could she not? He was so close, and she'd been thinking about the warmth of his embrace all day. Maybe they'd spend time together and they'd both realize they weren't each other's fate? Why not speed the process along?

And then Vi forgot about intellectual alibis and excuses to keep her distance from this man.

Chuck tasted of sweetness and the unknown. But a good kind of unknown.

He drew her into his lap with very little effort and let her kiss him for as long as she liked.

Which was a long time.

Chapter Seven

"I DON'T DO YOGA," VI SAID FOR WHAT SEEMED LIKE the tenth time.

"The goal of this week is to try new things." Grandma Dotty skipped down the front steps as Chuck pulled up in the black Town Car. "Yoga is good for your body and your mind."

"Don't be surprised if my mind falls asleep." Violet was tired. She'd stayed up too late kissing Chuck and she couldn't seem to find her regret this morning. "And since when did the week have a goal other than me getting my chapters done?"

"I like Dotty's goal." Chuck walked around the car and opened the door for her grandmother, giving her a friendly smile.

"You're supportive, Chuck." Grandma Dotty tweaked his cheek before getting in the back seat. "And reliable. All good qualities in a man."

Plus, he's a good kisser.

Chuck handed Vi a small cup of espresso. He didn't grin, but he looked at her with a gaze that said he was burning for her.

Violet's chest squeezed with happiness. Maybe Maggie and Chuck were right. Maybe she did need to let loose a little. Besides, it wasn't like Chuck was a celebrity or internet famous. He was just an average Joe, no threat to her position at Harvard.

Vi stared at her little coffee cup. "I'm not sure I should drink this. It might be better to fall asleep during yoga."

"You should drink it," Chuck whispered. "You never know about Dotty. She's under your watch and could slip out while you're sleeping in yoga class."

"How true that is." Vi gulped the espresso shots and then sat in the back seat, smiling like a fool falling in love.

"Go with the flow, Vi. Everybody does yoga now." Grandma Dotty was on a natural high, grinning at the world. "It helps in bed, I hear."

Vi choked on a breath. "To sleep, you mean?"

Grandma Dotty waved a hand. "You young kids can call it what you like."

Chuck slid behind the wheel. "What are we talking about?"

"Yoga flexibility and it's benefits in—"

"*Longevity!*" Vi shouted, cutting her grandmother off. "Everybody knows yoga practitioners lead long lives."

"Life is about balance." Chuck did a slow head-nod. "And yoga gives you balance."

"You do yoga?" Vi couldn't believe it.

"I don't do yoga classes, but I know many people who do."

"You should do yoga with us." Grandma Dotty clapped her hands. "Chuck is always so busy. And he's going to have to wait for us anyway."

"What a great idea." Vi teased, assuming Chuck wouldn't. And wouldn't his refusal to join them be good ammunition the next time he counseled her not to work so hard?

"I know when a gauntlet has been thrown." Chuck glanced at them over his shoulder. "Challenge accepted."

Violet's jaw dropped. "You're going to do yoga in your suit? No way."

"I have running shorts in back."

Oh, my.

Violet could only imagine how muscular those legs of his were.

～

"WELCOME TO YOGA FLOW." Kelcie sat on a mat at the front of the class with her legs criss crossed, pausing to welcome everyone with a warm smile.

Including Coop.

Dotty had jammed her mat in the front row. Predictably, Vivi had taken a spot at the back of class. And Coop had put down a mat right next to hers. He'd caught her looking at his legs once or twice.

It's going to be a good day.

"We'll be doing some gentle movements through different positions," Kelcie continued in a voice slower and more modulated than her usual bubbly, energetic way of talking. "Flowing through the class and noticing anything that might be sticky."

Sticky? Coop had Vivi stuck in his head.

"Let's move onto all fours." Kelcie started the yoga flowing, moving as she spoke. "And gently alternate between a high-arching cat and a low-belied cow stretch. Deep breaths in and out. Cat... And cow..."

"*Moo,*" Dotty said softly, although loud enough for the class to hear. "*Meow...*"

Vivi exhaled rather violently in what Coop considered the equivalent of a head-thunk.

"*Moo... Meow...*" Dotty said, louder this time.

Several people giggled.

"*Moo-ooo.*" Dotty gasped. "Kelcie, I'm stuck in the cow."

Kelcie got up to help her. "Let's move into a downward dog position."

"*Woof,*" Dotty said even though she was still on all fours.

Coop had to bite his lip to keep from laughing.

"*Hey,*" Vivi whispered, grinning. "Keep it moving. Downward dog."

Coop followed her lead.

"*Moo-woo-oof,*" Dotty sounded surprised as Kelcie tried to

shift her hips into the air for the downward dog position. "I'll just stay down here in the kitty-cow until we do an animal my body likes."

"Sure." Kelcie began walking between the mats. "Extend that right leg high into the air, really give that hip room to breathe."

Dotty grunted, indicating something was hard—whether it was the yoga position, or the breathing was unclear.

Coop had to peek. What if Dotty was in real trouble? Stuck in a pose or fallen over. But no. The elderly woman had moved from the cat-cow position into a frog position, which wasn't what Kelcie had called out.

"Bring that right leg around and through your arms and very gently lower yourself into a pigeon pose." Kelcie kept walking slowly between the mats, moving toward the back unaware of Dotty's frog predicament. "Find a comfortable stretch. Modify as needed."

"*Coo-coo.*" Dotty glanced at the woman next to her, trying to contort her body the way she was.

"Pigeon pose, Chuck." Kelcie stood at his mat until Coop achieved what was close to the required pose. She crossed the room and helped others adjust and align.

Coop glanced toward Vivi. He had no idea what she was doing, but it wasn't a pigeon pose. It looked more like a runner's stretch.

She noticed him watching her. "What?"

"You modified," he whispered. "I assumed a woman who walks for exercise would do yoga."

"Wrong again." She frowned at him. "Why do your legs bend like pretzels?"

Kelcie kneeled down between them. "Because he's a runner and he stretches."

Vivi's slender brows went up. "When do you have time to run?"

"Now. When people don't need a ride to sunrise yoga."

Kelcie tried to help Vivi into a pigeon pose, but the object of

Coop's affection had a body that didn't move that way. Finally, Kelcie gave up and moved on. "Let's shift to downward dog. Extend that left leg in the air... And move into pigeon pose on the other side."

"*Woof. Coo-coo,*" Dotty repeated the bird call.

Vivi gave up and curled up on the mat in what might have generously been a modified child's pose.

By the end of class, she was softly snoring.

So much for the espresso.

~

"TALLY, you need to work on your lead changes today." Coop saddled up the white mare.

"And her continuous lope, Chuckaroo," Rafi called from the front of the barn. "Stubborn horses always want to trot when they should be loping."

"Tally's not stubborn. She's opinionated. Aren't you, girl?" Coop patted her broad neck.

The mare nudged his chest with her nose. She was a good-natured horse, serving as a reminder that Coop shouldn't take his situation seriously every moment of the day.

He let her rub her forehead on his chest. "How goes the quest for a bank loan, Rafi?"

"Turned down again this week." He tossed a broken hinge he was removing on the ground. It clattered on the wood floor. "I'm going to be stuck here forever, Chuck-Chuck." He fit a new hinge on the stall door. "Not that it's a bad thing, I suppose. I've got another appointment with a different bank this afternoon."

"You'll get this one. And when you do, I'm going to replace you," Coop teased, although he had no plans to do so. "Is the apartment above the barn a two bedroom?"

"No. It's a studio."

There went Coop's hopes of renting a room from Rafi.

"Off we go to the arena, girl." Coop tightened Tally's girth strap before heading to the near barn door.

"Hey, no more Liberty training, Chucker," Rafi called after him. "I know Tally's a smart horse, but I don't want to have to tell Mrs. Finnegan that she escaped again."

"Right. No playing hooky today, darlin'."

"And no long, romantic beach rides either," Rafi added. "Mrs. Finnegan got wind of that, too. Let's stick to the arenas from now on. We both need these jobs."

"Right." Coop frowned. He'd hoped to ride a horse over to Vivi's place and check on her progress on the Shakespeare project. And maybe steal a kiss.

Steal wasn't the proper word. When he got close enough to Vivi, she tended to launch those sweet lips of hers in the direction of his face.

And I will not complain.

But Coop's frown didn't go away.

When they'd finished yoga this morning, Dotty had told Coop he owed her a ride. He'd given her his word. Coop didn't like to break a promise.

～

"Vi!" Grandma Dotty rushed out to the patio and sat in a chair next to Violet. She wore bright pink leggings and a gray swing blouse. "Do you have a second?"

"Sure." Violet's fingers had been drumming the keys for several minutes without typing any words. It was almost a relief to remove them from the vicinity of her laptop.

"Watch me dance." And without turning on any music, her grandmother stood and began a frenetic set of movements that Vi was hard-pressed to identify.

"Wow," Violet said dutifully. "Nice." In truth, it was better than anything she could do.

Grandma Dotty stopped, panting and red-cheeked. "It's good, right?"

"It's something." Vi nodded. "Did Kelcie teach you that today?"

"No." Smiling, her grandmother pulled the hem of her swing blouse side-to-side. She looked blissful. "I was watching one of those morning talk shows, and they had a performance by a hip hop singer."

"Did they? What was his name?"

"It was a *her.*" Grandma Dotty pinched her features in concentration. "Kitty Cat? Bitty Cat? No. Lola Cat?"

"Doja Cat?" It was a good guess, even though the artist considered herself a rapper.

"That's her!" Grandma Dotty threw a couple more dance moves with age-defying velocity. "I stole her steps. And she gave me an idea for my Xuri audition costume."

"Okay. That sounds great." And it was. Truly, it was. When Grandma Dotty was happy, it was as if the world was a more beautiful and exciting place. If only some of that transferred to Violet's book. She was about ready to skip the chapter on fate altogether and move on to the chapter on familial relationships in Shakespeare's works.

Violet's laptop screen went black, entering sleep mode.

And maybe that's what Violet needed, too. Sleep. A nice nap instead of sitting out here waiting for a words to come or a man to show.

Chapter Eight

"We're seriously going to race horses on the beach?" Dotty didn't wait for Coop to confirm. She clapped her hands and then threw herself into his arms beneath the trees separating the Summer property from the beach.

"I see where you get your enthusiasm from," Coop said to Vivi over Dotty's head, holding onto a trio of reins. "Throwing yourself at men must be a Summer female trait."

Vivi crossed her arms over her chest and gave Coop a look that denied his theory. "And thus ends the streak you've experienced of me making the first move."

Coop didn't believe for a minute that she wouldn't lip-bomb him again.

"Are you two dating?" Dotty stared up at Coop, squinting.

"Not yet." He set Dotty aside. "Ladies, let's mount up and have this beachy horse race."

Coop had taken the trio of horses without permission as soon as Rafi had left Beeswax Farm. He wanted to be back long before his boss returned.

"Dotty, you'll be riding I Dunno." He handed her the reins to a dun gelding. "Vivi, you're riding Papi." He handed her the reins to a palomino mare and kept the reins to Tally for himself.

"Give me a boost, Chuck." Dotty lifted her left foot mere inches off the ground.

He bent, grabbed her by the waist, and lifted her in the air. She weighed next to nothing.

Dotty slipped her foot in the stirrup and flung herself into the saddle like a pro. "On your marks. Get set. Go!" And off she went, galloping toward the beach.

"You snooze, you lose, cowboy." Vivi shot off on Papi.

Coop hopped on Tally and made after them, crying, "*Cheaters!*"

Down on the beach, Dotty led the pack, bouncing in the saddle like she was on a pogo stick. She rode the way she did everything else—with one hundred and ten percent effort and two hundred percent glee. She whooped it up, guiding the dun to the wet sand and showing no fear.

Vivi rode at a controlled gallop in her grandmother's wake. She had a graceful seat and a light hand on the reins. Papi tossed her head as the last vestiges of a gentle wave churned at her feet. Vivi slowed the pace to an easy lope.

It wasn't long before Coop caught up to Vivi. The smell of the salt air. The warmth of the afternoon sun. The occasional splash of horse hooves in water. Some people dreamed of moments like this.

Riding side-by-side, Vivi and Coop exchanged a smile. Coop was more convinced than ever that Vivi was his everything.

Far ahead, Dotty pulled I Dunno to a stop with a spray of sand. She turned the horse around and trotted back to them, bouncing all the way. Not that it seemed to matter to her. She grinned from ear-to-ear. "I won!"

"There was never any doubt," Vivi told her. And then she looked at Coop. "Thank you for this. It was on her bucket list. She's so proud of that list and all her accomplishments."

"There are plenty of ways you can thank me later," he teased.

As expected, Vivi blushed and rolled her eyes. "Can we ride further down the beach? It's such a beautiful day."

He refrained from making any jokes about Shakespeare waiting for her back at the house.

"I say yes. Let's keep riding." Dotty reached them and turned the dun around, bringing the gelding next to Coop. She sat the walking horse as if she'd been in the saddle since birth, a contrary image to her bouncy seat at a gallop. "Who's up for another race?"

"No!" both Coop and Vivi said.

Dotty sniffed. "I would have won anyway."

Coop and Vivi let her think that by keeping silent.

"What are you going to do with your life, Chuck?" Dotty asked, seemingly out of the blue. "Are you one of those drifters whose only dream is to be internet famous and lazily wealthy?"

"*Grandma.*"

Dotty leaned forward to catch Vivi's eye. "If he's serious about you, I'm allowed to ask. Driving cars and exercising horses should be a means to something else."

"*Grandma.*"

"No. It's okay." Coop certainly understood where the old gal was coming from. She wanted the best for Vivi. "I want to help people." That thought had been forming for the last few days. "I want to make a difference in the lives of people." Rafi's chipper face came to mind. "And help make their dreams come true."

"And how will you do that?" Dotty looked puzzled. "Work at an amusement park? Build fancy swimming pools? Or..."

Coop shook his head at her examples. "If I knew the how, I wouldn't be wasting my time driving and riding, would I?"

"True that." Dotty nodded approvingly. "I've often said it takes men longer to mature than women. How old are you? Thirty? That's a good time to get your life on track."

"I'm thirty-five."

Dotty sat back, giving Coop a dramatic once-over. "Geez, you're behind. Do you have an excuse? Did you serve in the military? Battle a severe illness?"

"No. None of that." Coop wished he could tell the Summer

women the truth, but what would that serve? He'd still look like a slacker.

"You could work for a charity," Vivi suggested.

"Chuck!" Rafi stood on the bank of Beeswax Farm, looking none too happy. "I've been looking all over for you."

Uh-oh.

"Hey, Rafi." Coop turned Tally toward the bank.

The two Summer women followed suit.

"I told you not to take the horses out to the beach." The normally even-keeled Rafi sounded hot under the collar. He tipped his cowboy hat back. "Mrs. Finnegan noticed some horses were missing and called me back from the feed store. What were you thinking?"

"That he'd help check off an old woman's bucket list," Dotty said unhelpfully. "My dream, that is."

Rafi's expression darkened.

"I'm sorry," Coop hurried to say. "It was just a short ride. It won't happen again."

"Darn right, it won't." Rafi came down the bank, hand outstretched, impatient for them to give him the reins. "Ride's over. Everybody off."

Coop dismounted and helped Dotty get off of I Dunno. Vivi was silent as she gave Rafi her mount's reins. The breeze had died, and the sun beat down on them, hot and stifling.

Rafi snatched the leather pair of reins from Coop's hand. "I know you're hustling for a buck, man. But this isn't right. Ladies, make sure you tip your guide. He's going to need the extra cash because he's no longer employed at Beeswax Farm."

Vivi gasped.

The gravity of Coop's mistake buzzed in his ears. He wasn't just in need of a place to stay. Now he needed to find another job. "Rafi, is this really necessary? Can't we talk about this?"

"Don't fire him, Mr. Rafi. He's not our guide." Despite latching onto Coop's arm, Dotty sounded miles away. "He's our limo driver."

"Whatever he is, don't rely on him." Rafi frowned at Coop. "He never listens. He acts like he owns this place." He turned and led the horses away. "But the truth is, he doesn't *know* his place."

"Rafi, come on, man. Let me explain." Coop made to follow his friend.

Vivi grabbed onto his other arm. "Let him go. There's nothing to gain when tempers flare."

Coop took a moment to consider her advice before nodding. "I'll walk you home."

"No. We're fine." Vivi released him and took her grandmother by the hand. "You have a lot to think about. Not just about this job. But about your family and your future."

He wanted to argue, to tell her that this job didn't matter in the long run. But the truth was that he'd never been fired before. It was shaming.

Coop watched the two ladies go with a heavy heart. And then he turned and trudged back to the barn at Beeswax Farm. And all the while, his thoughts circled around the type of man he was now and the man he wanted to be in the future.

I don't take orders well.

If he was being honest, he took the duties Rafi had given him as more like suggestions that didn't necessarily need to be obeyed.

My behavior impacts more than just me.

Rafi had been called back to deal with Coop's behavior. He might be at risk of being fired, too.

Do I have what it takes to be a good leader if I can't be a good employee?

Coop doubted it. But he could be. Someday.

There was a lesson to be learned here. But first, he needed to apologize to Rafi and Mrs. Finnegan, the owner of Beeswax Farm.

～

"I ORDERED AN UBER," Violet said to Grandma Dotty as a familiar black Lincoln Town Car pulled into the driveway Friday morning. It had been two days since she'd seen Chuck. And now this.

"Only Chuck will do for me," Grandma Dotty said in her most determined voice. "Get out your phone and delete the other driver. I didn't like the guy who drove us yesterday morning."

"Delete the other driver," Vi mumbled. "You mean, cancel the ride?"

"Yes, whatever." Her grandmother skipped down the steps. "Chuck needs our support, and we need someone who knows our routine with hip hop cardio."

Violet opened the ride share app on her phone and cancelled the car she'd ordered. The fog hung above them as gray as her mood. Chuck had made a foolish mistake the other day, taking out horses that weren't his to give them a ride. No wonder his father wanted him to think seriously about his future. Vi couldn't afford to have a relationship with a man like that.

"Good morning, ladies." Chuck opened the car door for Grandma Dotty with one hand. In the other, he held a small paper coffee cup with what was presumably Vi's morning espresso.

Violet wanted that espresso like nobody's business. She'd spent two nights tossing and turning. She wanted Chuck to be as steady in his work life as he seemed to be in his interest toward her.

"I made a mistake," Chuck said humbly, extending a hand with her espresso. "I'm sorry. Not only did I disappoint my employer, I let myself and those who believe in me down, too."

Vi nodded. It was the right thing to say. "I accept your apology and your espresso. But..." She stopped on the other side of the car door from him, taking the cup while being careful not to touch his hand. "This has only proved what I've been saying all along. We should just be...friends."

His expression turned stony. Those cheekbones stiffened. His eyes didn't sparkle. His mouth didn't grin mischievously.

And she missed his irreverence. His upbeat demeanor. His interest in her.

Violet sat in the car feeling sad and hollow. The easy camaraderie they'd experienced earlier in the week was painfully missing. And the worst part of it was that she'd be here for weeks to come with Grandma Dotty calling on Chuck to provide them with transportation.

For a brief moment, she considered buying or renting a car. Converting her grandmother to using the ride sharing apps would be more financially sound.

Chuck closed Vi's door and came around to the driver's seat.

"Why is everyone so glum today?" Grandma Dotty finger-combed her hair into an upright, haystack position. "It's not like Chuck's lost career as a stable boy is a tragedy. He's destined for bigger things. This is just a sign."

"That's a nice way to put it." Chuck didn't so much as glance in the rear view mirror.

"I'm a nice person," Grandma Dotty said. "But so is Vi. Go on, Vi. You tell him."

"Beeswax Farm isn't your..." She'd been about to say destiny. Instead, she substituted, "...fate."

"And here we go," Chuck muttered. After a moment, he sighed and caught Vi's gaze in the rear view mirror. "I don't want to fight about what I did or what my fate is."

"That makes two of us," Violet said.

"Three," added Grandma Dotty.

"Someday soon, I'd like to sit down and explain everything." Chuck slid on a pair of dark glasses.

Grandma Dotty leaned over toward Vi. "Why can't he explain himself now? We have a nice car ride there and back."

"That's what I was wondering," Vi told her. "I guess it's just not something we can understand easily."

Chuck grunted in the front seat. Possibly in agreement?

"Vi, we need to really work on our game today at hip hop cardio." Her grandmother was in full distraction mode today. "I hear Xuri is back for the weekend and planning something huge. This is my chance."

Yes, but it wasn't Vi's chance. She didn't want to be a hip hop runway model. She'd wanted to be loved by a stable man who still knew how to have a good time. Not a good time charmer who had no clue about what to do with his life.

Chapter Nine

"WE'RE PARTYING TONIGHT." WEARING XURI'S WHITE, puffy jacket, Grandma Dotty practiced her hip hop moves late Friday afternoon.

And the funny thing was that after a week of private lessons and hip hop cardio classes, she was starting to look good in that oversized white denim coat. That was the silver lining to this week, Vi had decided while going through the motions in their hip hop cardio class that morning. Grandma Dotty might just check another box off her bucket list—be a runway model.

But a party...

Vi wasn't in a party mood.

She was working at the kitchen table. She closed her laptop. "Who invited us to this party?"

"Marguerite from hip hop cardio. She and Xuri are close because Marguerite buys the complete collection every year." Her grandmother wiped the back of her jacket back and forth over her behind, presumably shaking her tail feather. "I hear Marguerite's party is just to screen who gets invited to the after party. And then there's a big mystery about the after-after party. We can't miss out on the after-after party."

"Stop." Violet removed her reading glasses and channeled her father's sternest voice. "We can only go to one party. You do remember that you like to go to bed at nine. It's why you pop out of bed in the morning before six."

Grandma Dotty's mouth made a little o. "You don't want to be social and dance?"

"I don't."

"But this is my chance to show Xuri that people of all ages can model for her." She flipped her hood up over her head. It dropped into place and covered her eyes and nose. "You don't have to go to the after parties. I'll attend alone."

Violet was struck by a wave of fear. Unless in New York City, her grandmother rarely went anywhere unchaperoned, certainly not on the party circuit. "No going solo."

"Vi, I'm a grown woman and—"

"Don't make me call Dad." Not that Vi wanted to call him either. But she needed an iron clad argument.

Grandma Dotty lifted her head, but half her face was still covered by blue-gray faux fur. "I didn't think you were like your father and saw me as a little old lady in her twilight years. Would you like to be viewed that way? I mean, what would Shakespeare think about me enjoying life while you read about make-believe characters written over five hundred years ago?"

Low blow.

Violet got to her feet and came around the table. She carefully tipped Grandma Dotty's hood back so that she could look her in the eye. "I get it. This is *The Taming of the Shrew*. You're Bianca, beloved by all, and I'm Kate, the party-pooping shrew."

The life of the party crossed her arms over her chest and thrust her nose in the air. "Well, if the shoe fits."

"*Grandma.*" Even though it was Vi's metaphor, the fact that her grandmother agreed stung.

"*Violet.*" Her grandmother took Violet's hands and gave them a shake. "I have a chance to prove to something to Xuri and myself. But to do that, I have to be able to hang with the in-crowd. And I'll do it regardless if it's one party, two, or three."

She made a good case. And yet, Vi suspected that a night on the party circuit with her grandmother wouldn't end well. But it was hard to turn her grandmother down when there was such an earnest plea in her eyes.

How much trouble could a sweet little old lady get into during a night of revelry in the Hamptons?

Violet sighed.

History said she could get in a lot of trouble. Just ask Violet's siblings and cousins. "If I do this, will you take a day off from your model-training regimen? Can I have one day without sweaty, pretzel-twisting interruptions to work on my book?" She should make more progress now that she had no kissing distractions, but it was as if she had a relationship hangover. And they hadn't even been dating!

"Vi, you have a deal." Her grandmother practically glowed. She held up her fingers as if she was making a Girl Scout pledge. "We'll sleep in over the weekend. That's not one day. It's two. And I will be so quiet that you won't even know I'm here."

"But you will be here," Violet felt compelled to add, because she knew a dodgy reply when she heard one. And this sounded like her grandmother had plans to go somewhere else.

"I'll always be right where you can find me," Grandma Dotty said cagily.

And no matter how hard Violet tried to pin her down, that was as close to a promise of being house-bound as she could get.

It was going to be a long night, but hopefully, not a long weekend.

⁓

COOP SHOWED up at eight o'clock on Friday night to pick up the Summer ladies and take them to a party. The sun was low in the horizon and the air was hot and muggy.

He'd heard there was a series of parties hosted by Dotty's favorite designer this weekend, and all of them were rumored to be wild. The monied crowd could party ugly, something he hadn't acknowledged until he'd been one of the help. He wasn't happy about Dotty and Vivi going. But what could he do? Vivi had shut him out.

He liked the evening even less when Vivi walked down the front steps in a swanky little black dress and delicate high-heeled sandals. Her hair fell in nearly-tamed brown curls over her shoulders. And her eyes were luminous, seemingly larger than usual when highlighted by artfully applied, bold make-up.

Did she look like this a week ago when I swept her off her feet? He didn't think so.

"You ladies look beautiful." He held the car door open for them to get in. "Maybe I should go inside the party with you to beat the men back."

"Naw." Dotty patted his cheek before getting in, smelling of rose water and face powder. She wore a loose-fitting silver sheath beneath a white denim gangster jacket, undoubtedly the Xuri coat she'd been talking about dancing in all week. "I know Kung Fu. Or is that Feng Shui?" She slid across the seat to make room for Vivi.

"Definitely Feng Shui." Vivi joked, moving with the kind of grace he'd expect from a New York City heiress, exhibiting none of the early morning exercise frump he was so fond of. She smelled of exotic flowers and fancy fundraisers. He wanted his grumpy, wildflower-smelling professor back.

Coop walked slowly around the car to get in.

"You should go back in and get your purse," Vivi was saying.

"I don't need a purse. I have all these deep pockets." Dotty flapped the ends of her coat. "I have my cell phone in there and twenty dollars mad money."

"A twenty won't get you much," Vivi pointed out.

"You'd be surprised at what a twenty can get you on a Friday night," Dotty quipped.

Vivi pressed her deep red lips together.

Oh, there was tension in the car. Coop pulled out, rolling past the lushly landscaped grounds.

"Is this your anniversary ring?" Vivi grabbed her grandmother's hand, looking and sounding horrified. "That's supposed to be in a safe back in New York City."

"It's in the safe when it's not on my finger." Dotty nodded. "I know the combination to your father's safe. I can take this ring wherever and whenever I want to. It's mine." She raised her hand and executed a princess wave.

Coop's mouth hung open. The rock on her finger was as large as a candy jaw-breaker. He'd assumed the Summer family had money. But he hadn't thought they'd had the kind of money that diamond ring promised.

"The last time you wore that ring, you nearly poked your eye out," Vivi was saying.

"I'll be careful," Dotty promised.

"While you're dancing?" Vivi wasn't sold.

Dotty huffed.

Vivi huffed back.

They were quiet the rest of the drive to the party.

Coop pulled up to a sprawling mansion off the main drag in town. The party was already in full swing. Music blared into the fast approaching twilight. But before he dropped off his passengers, Coop had to get near the driveway. Unfortunately, whoever was hosting the party had hired valet parking, as was common for the bigger events. And the line for the valet seemed backed up into the street.

A young staffer wearing black slacks and a red polo shirt with a car logo stitched over his chest approached the Town Car. "Can we park this for you?" The teenager had a pen and ticket stub at the ready. With the acne and the braces, he didn't look old enough to drive.

"Sorry, kid. I need to take them to the front door."

"No one drives down the driveway but staff," the kid told Coop with more than a hint of Hampton snark.

I used to be like him.

Two months ago, he'd carried the monied chip on his shoulder like a badge of honor. Now that he'd struggled to make ends meet, had been fired and was soon to be evicted, he just thought of it as the mark of an entitled jerk.

"They want to park your car," Dotty told him. "That's a sign, Chuck. And since you're our driver, that means you can tag along to the party with us."

Yes!

Maybe this was fate intervening and helping him patch things up with Vivi.

"Peachy," Vivi said with an endearing dose of her morning grump. "Because now it's two against one, Grandma Dotty."

"Yes." Dotty sniffed, nose in the air. "Chuck and me against you."

Coop thought he heard Vivi make a primal sound, much like a growl.

"Let's go have some fun." Valet ticket in his pocket, Coop offered each woman an arm. Together, they walked down the crowded driveway and ascended the grand front steps to the extremely loud party.

Coop didn't want to go in. He'd much rather sit in a quiet place with Vivi and share a frozen yogurt.

"They're dancing out by the pool," Dotty shouted before working her way through the crowd. Her coat acted like a set of football pads. She probably didn't feel any of the shoulders, hips or elbows she bumped into. Likewise, those who were slow to get out of her path probably didn't feel the jab of her elbow either.

"Nice technique," Coop said in a loud voice. He took hold of Vivi's hand and made to follow.

"She learned that shopping the clearance sales at Bergdorf's," Vivi shouted from behind him.

Coop was too broad shouldered to zip in between the guests the way Dotty did. It wasn't long before they lost sight of her. Bodies pressed against them. He saw a gap in the wall and drew

Vivi inside a nook with a small desk. "Let's regroup. We'll catch up to Dotty soon enough."

Vivi's forehead furrowed with worry.

He brushed his thumb over the lines, smoothing them out. "You've got this. And you've got me. I know my life looks like a trainwreck, but I've got this. All of it." And in that moment, Coop believed it was true. He knew what he wanted to do with his life and how he fit into the Pearson family. All he needed was a formal plan and his father's approval.

Coop bent to kiss those sweet red lips of Vivi's—because she was close, staring at his mouth, and they were alone in a sea of people. Her lips were warm and welcoming. He wrapped his arms around her and deepened the kiss, drawing her close, wondering how he was going to tell her that he wasn't who she thought he was.

Vivi drew back, gaze searching his.

"What's wrong?"

"You went somewhere. Right in the middle of kissing me." She arched those expressive brows.

And he wished they didn't need to find Dotty. He wished they were truly alone. "I need to tell you something." The time had come.

"*Chuck!*" Kelcie practically fell into the nook with them. She grabbed hold of Coop's arm at the wrist above the hand that held onto the woman he'd been kissing. With one mercenary glance at Vivi, Kelcie yanked Coop's arm free and turned him around. "You need to try this new drink."

Vivi slipped away, presumably to follow Dotty.

"No. I don't." He dug in his heels, craning his neck to track Vivi's progress. Impossible. The crowd was too dense.

"But Chuck. It's super tingly." Kelcie held up a tumbler with pink and white liquid swirling in it. "And everything seems so much better after you drink one."

He suspected there was more in her drink than alcohol. Her pupils were dilated. He plucked the drink from of her hands and set it down on a side table. "I'm working tonight. Driving." He held out his hands as if he gripped a steering wheel in case she couldn't hear. "No drinks for me. I need to find Dotty and Vivi." Especially since there were suspect drinks in the house.

"O.M.G.! Dotty is so fun. She and I are going to be runway models for Xuri." Kelcie lurched sideways, face suddenly sweaty and turning a sickening green.

"You need some air." And luckily, if Dotty had been heading for the pool, there'd be plenty of it. Coop took Kelcie by the arm and made his way slowly to the backyard.

The party was less of a crush outside, but it was still difficult to navigate through. Coop spotted Dotty's coat on the far side of the pool. A blond man was talking to Vivi halfway between Coop and Dotty. She laughed at whatever he said.

Simon. The air whooshed from Coop's chest in a dash of jealousy and fear. He hadn't told Vivi who he was, and he didn't want Simon to blab the truth about him. He needed time to tell her and a way to ease into it gently. He was just beginning to repair the damage his firing had caused. Vivi may not give him a second chance.

He hurried down the stairs, dragging a now silent Kelcie after him. When he finally reached Vivi, the man who'd been moving in on his territory turned.

"Coop!" Simon clapped a hand on his shoulder. "I knew we'd run into each other again."

Vivi frowned at him. "*Coop?*"

If Coop didn't say something fast, Simon was going to blow everything. "Simon, I have someone I want you to meet." He dragged Kelcie forward and introduced her.

There was a dull look in Kelcie's eye, but she smiled a little. And she looked cute in her purple dress, her blond hair a mass of curls. Simon liked blondes. And Kelcie managed a wave. "I run the local *boot* camps." Only she didn't say *boot.* "Oops." Kelcie placed her palms over her bra cups and jiggled the goods. "Boosh camp...Book camp...boo-oo..."

"She's an exercise instructor," Vivi came to her rescue. "Her talent is smiling while making my muscles scream in agony."

All this was shouted, because the music blared at rock concert levels. Coop could have sworn the empty pool had waves made by the beat of the bass.

"Yep." Kelcie massaged her cheeks and lips the way one did after getting a shot of Novocain.

"Hey, Simon." Coop guided Kelcie next to him. "We need to retrieve Vivi's grandmother. Can you watch Kelcie? She's had too much to drink."

"One drink." Kelcie's arm shot straight up in the air, index finger pointing toward the wisps of pinkish-tinged clouds. "Chuck discarded my second glass."

Coop didn't wait to see if Simon agreed to babysit or if Kelcie protested. He took Vivi's hand and made his way to the end of the pool, tugging her along. Except... "Where did Dotty go?" The huge coat with blue bunnies was nowhere to be seen.

"There!" Vivi pointed toward a gazebo.

Sure enough, the elderly dynamo had found space in the gazebo overlooking the ocean.

Weaving in and around party-goers, it took them another few minutes to get to her.

Darn crowd.

"Do you have any water?" Dotty asked when they reached her. She'd removed her big, white denim coat and had set it on a nearby chair. "All this dancing in this heat...I'm parched." She fanned herself with her hand.

"You scratched yourself." Vivi rushed in, wetting her thumb with her mouth and then wiping away the thin streak of blood on Dotty's cheek. "I told you that ring was dangerous. Where is it?"

"In my jacket pocket." Dotty waved a hand in the direction of her coat. "Along with my cell phone and that twenty. I'm parched. Flag down a passing waiter, will you?"

Not wanting Dotty to receive a spiked drink and needing a

few minutes to frame his explanation for hiding his true identity, Coop volunteered to get the old girl a glass of water.

When he returned to the gazebo several minutes later, Simon and Kelcie had joined Vivi and Dotty. Coop's gut clenched. The music was too loud, and he was too panicked to have rehearsed what to say to Vivi about his true identity.

"Coop." Simon clapped him on the back, making Coop spill some of Dotty's water.

"That's twice he's called you that." Vivi crossed her arms over her chest. There was an accusation and vulnerability in her eyes. She didn't like to be disappointed or lied to. He wouldn't have either. "I knew you weren't a *Chuck*."

"I can explain," Coop said, handing Dotty her water. He drew Vivi a few steps away from the others.

"I want to hear, too." Dotty followed, drinking from her water glass. "He's my favorite limo driver."

"Limo driver?" Simon nudged his way in the circle between Vivi and Coop. "He's the most eligible bachelor in the south. He might be more famous than I am. Plus, he comes from Texas oil money. The real deal. He doesn't need to work a day in his life."

"I can explain," Coop repeated.

"Not work?" Dotty laughed. "Chuck's been driving us around for days."

"And he was crushed when Beeswax Farm fired him," Vivi said, looking dubiously at Coop. "Is it true? Are you wealthy? And...and a celebrity of sorts?"

"Yes and no." Coop could tell she was worried about his reputation marring her chances for tenure at Harvard. He reached for Vivi, trying to draw her closer. "Can we talk somewhere in private?"

Vivi moved away, out of reach. "We don't need privacy. We need honesty. And that's something you should have no problem letting everyone hear."

"I don't get it." Kelcie glanced up at Simon. "Did Chuck change his name?"

"He has many names," Simon said with a suddenly sympathetic glance at Coop. "He has many names, just like I do. Let's give them a minute." He led the fitness instructor a few feet away, coming around behind the gazebo and the chair where Dotty had left her coat, earning Coop's forgiveness for spilling the beans about who he was in the first place.

Heartened because Vivi hadn't left him, Coop chose his words carefully. "I told you about my father, Vivi. About what he told me to do."

"He wanted you to find something to do other than..." Vivi gestured toward the crowded house and pool. She took a few steps out of the gazebo. "Oil? I thought he owned a garage or a local jewelry store or something. I thought he sent you, his hardworking son, out to find himself. Not—"

"I've been on my own for two months. Working any job I could find. And trying to figure out my future." Coop followed her. "And for the record, Chuck is a nickname for Charles, my first name. My Texas friends know me as Coop, short for my middle name—Cooper."

"You lied to me. Oil... You being famous..." Her fingers hovered over her lips. "I have no idea who I was...*with*."

"I didn't lie," he hurried to say. "I am Chuck *and* Coop. Just like you're Violet and Vi and Vivi."

"I am *not* Vivi." Brown eyes blazing, her hands landed on her hips. "And to think I was falling for you. Nothing about you is real."

"I'm real," he stated in a calm voice. "And what you feel for me is real, whether you call me Chuck or Coop or Shakespeare."

"I'm not going to call you anything!" Vivi's eyes teared up.

His heart sank, but he refused to leave her side and shy away from her disappointed stare.

Someone shouted unintelligible words.

"Did you hear that? They're calling for dancers." Dotty glanced about, not that there was much to see beyond the packed party-goers. "Where did Kelcie disappear to?"

"She's with Simon." Coop turned around. Except Kelcie wasn't standing next to Simon. Worry elbowed angst over things with Vivi aside. Kelcie was in no shape to be wandering around alone. "Simon, where did she go?"

"She said she needed a drink." Simon looked up from his phone, scanning their surroundings.

"I see Xuri on the steps leading down to the pool," Dotty said excitedly. She handed Coop her water glass. "I'm off for my modeling audition." She turned, facing the chairs in the gazebo, both of which were empty. "Where's my coat? I set it down right here."

"Your ring." Vivi paled, staring at the empty chairs.

Coop, Simon, and Vivi immediately mobilized and searched the area, including the bushes and grounds in a ten foot radius. But the coat had disappeared. Apparently, along with Kelcie.

The mass of attendees thickened, crowding around the pool where Xuri and an entourage of black-clad, ultra-thin models struck poses. The music faded away.

"Party people," Xuri said in a loud, grating voice. "This is your chance to catch my attention."

"Like anyone could dance in this throng." Coop scoffed as the band began playing something that sounded like hip hop.

"I'm missing my audition." Dotty looked like she might cry. "Xuri can't see me without the coat, not in this crowd."

"Here." Coop removed his black suit jacket, plucking his cell phone free of the interior pocket. "You can do your dance audition for Xuri wearing my coat. We'll clear you some space."

The elderly woman eyed it with distaste.

"We can make this work." Vivi took Coop's jacket and helped her grandmother into it. She rolled up the sleeves and turned up the coat collar. "Summer women don't give up."

"You're right. I'm going to make my way to Xuri and dance in her face." Dotty fluffed her short gray hair. "Wish me luck." She strutted off toward the other end of the pool with a hip-swaying attitude experienced runway models would envy.

"Hey!" Vivi pointed. "There's her coat."

Sure enough. A woman wearing Dotty's coat weaved her way through the crowd toward Xuri, hood up so they couldn't see her face. The rest of her body was hidden by Xuri's audience.

Vivi darted off, heading for trouble with Coop at her high heels.

"Since when do you ride shotgun for damsels in distress?" Simon tried to walk at Coop's shoulder. "Your interest in women doesn't last beyond a date or two."

"I'm not that guy anymore, Simon." He was Chuck. Or Shakespeare.

Just a hardworking man that a hardworking woman needed.

Chapter Ten

A LIE. A WICKED LIE.

The real Shakespeare would rail at her kissing cowboy's deception.

Violet had no time to throw a fit or tell Cowboy/Chuck/Shakespeare/Coop what a rat turd he was for pretending to be something he wasn't. She had to be her grandmother's wingman and get her coat back before her grandmother's priceless ring went permanently missing.

She jostled someone as she passed. "Sorry." She kept moving, kept bumping into people, kept apologizing. She passed by four, five, ten people and whoever had Grandma Dotty's coat on was still the same distance ahead of her.

The partiers made room for Xuri. The designer strutted down the steps toward the pool deck in ridiculously high, black platform pumps. Her dress was a collection of colorful ribbons sewn to a sheer, thigh-length sheath. She wore a black bowler cap over a blond wig and used a cane as a third leg to navigate through the crowd, tapping partiers with it to get them out of her way to the pool.

A few people were trying to audition, performing hip hop

moves, dancing aggressively in tight quarters. Perhaps too aggressively. Someone got punched in the face and a fight erupted. A woman was shoved into a cluster of people, and they all went down like dominoes.

Forget saving Grandma Dotty's ring, Violet had to save Grandma Dotty!

"I think Kelcie stole the coat," Chuck, or whatever his name was, said from behind Vi.

"Whoever stole the coat will be sorry once my grandmother catches her. One time at Bergdorf's, she got into a tug of war over the last pair of sandals on clearance." Security had been called. "But you don't need to worry about us. I'll protect her." If only she wasn't still twenty feet away.

"We still need to talk after this is over."

Violet glanced back at Chuck/Coop. His friend Simon was right behind him, stuck on her cowboy chauffeur like a fake nail to a freshly buffed fingernail. "No." It was one thing to fall for a blue collar man who was trying to get his life together and another to fall for a man who came from a family like she did, one that sometimes was newsworthy. "It's bad enough that you're a notorious playboy, but Xuri is a notorious attention-seeker. After this is over, my grandmother and I are going to ground." Vi just hoped she could get out of this mess without any media attention.

Voices rose behind her. Violet turned.

"It's my coat! And I *will* have it back!" That was Grandma Dotty's most determined voice.

"I'm just borrowing it." Those slurred words sounded like Kelcie.

Grandma Dotty had her hands on one arm of her stolen coat and was trying to tug it off Kelcie. But several of Xuri's models were grabbing onto the coat from behind Kelcie or were trying to grab hold of Grandma Dotty, who was balanced precariously on the pool edge coping.

Chuck/Coop edged past Violet, heading toward the ruckus.

"This isn't your coat, old lady," said a pompous-looking young man with chiseled facial features. He was dressed all in black, standing behind Kelcie. He held onto Grandma Dotty's jacket at the shoulders. "Let go!"

"You mind your manners, sonny boy." Grandma Dotty's face was pinched with determination. Her efforts increased. "You just want the coat for yourself."

Xuri smiled, circled by her little minions.

"I just want my chance, Dotty." Kelcie was being shaken like a rag doll by Grandma Dotty and the man behind her.

As for the jacket...

It was either going to rip or end up with whoever had a stronger grip.

Vi's fear for her grandmother's safety increased to breath-stealing levels. But what could she do?

Nothing, except hope that Chuck/Coop could reach her grandmother soon.

A hand settled on Violet's waist. A proprietary touch. She jumped, and half-turned, so on edge that she nearly lost her balance and fell.

"We should try to get closer," Simon shouted in her ear.

First Chuck/Coop wooed her with his smooth moves and now his buddy was making a play?

Frustration coiled in Vi's shoulders. Anger roared in her ears.

"Now isn't the time for a pass!" Violet spun the rest of the way around and pushed Simon back.

He fell into the pool.

Oops.

As one, the crowd seemed to shut up and turn toward the splash. Vi used the distraction to push onward.

But the commotion threw Grandma Dotty and her adversaries off. Grandma Dotty's balance wavered. She released the coat. Her arms cartwheeled and her little booty pushed back-and-forth as she tried to find her equilibrium.

"No!" Vi shouted, trying to push her way through the swarm.

"Really, Violet?" Simon was a bad swimmer, arms splashing clumsily as he swam past. "I was only trying to help you reach your grandmother!"

"A likely story, Mr. Handsy," someone nearby said, giving Violet a thumbs up.

I'm going to have to apologize to Simon later.

Just then, Grandma Dotty went over backward into the pool. "*I-eee!*"

"Dotty!" Kelcie slipped free of the jacket and tumbled after Grandma Dotty jacket-less, just as Chuck/Coop reached her.

A wave of water drenched his legs.

Violet tried to move forward, but the crowd was packed solid with onlookers just as eager for a gander at the unfolding events as she was to come to her grandmother's rescue.

"Give me that." Chuck/Coop reached for Dotty's jacket, but the interfering model wearing black yanked it out of reach and one of his buddies shoved Chuck/Coop in the pool.

"Help!" Grandma Dotty cried, gasping for air as Kelcie screamed and tried to climb on top of her.

"Chuck! Coop! Kelcie's drowning my grandmother." Violet tried once more to cut through the crowd.

"I'm coming." Simon swam slowly past Violet.

"I've got this." Chuck/Coop pulled Kelcie into his arms, leaving Simon to assist Grandma Dotty.

Her grandmother wasn't eager for Simon's brand of help. "Young man, you're an octopus. Get your hands off me!"

"O.M.G. He's a perv," someone nearby said, giving rise to more unflattering comments about Simon.

"He's just trying to help," Vi said in poor Simon's defense.

The fashionable crush began inching away from the pool deck, giving it a wide berth. A couple of men in khaki shorts and polo shirts set down their drinks and helped those who'd taken a dunking out of the pool. Marguerite, who was renting the house and had invited Grandma Dotty, showed up with beach towels.

"Where's my jacket?" Grandma Dotty demanded as Violet

helped dry her off. "I see Xuri inside. I still have a chance to audition but she's heading for the door."

"Can we push pause on the pursuit of your modeling career for a minute?" Violet bent to look her grandmother in the eye. "What does Dad say about arguing in public?"

Grandma Dotty's nose went in the air. "I kindly requested Kelcie return my coat."

"I was just gonna wear it to dance in front of Xuri." Kelcie's lower lip stuck out. There was a sickly sheen to her face and a glazed look in her eyes. "You told me you'd help me. And I thought we could take turns."

"I..." Something wild gathered in Grandma Dotty's expression. "There is no *I* in team, you backstabber!"

"Give her a pass, Dotty," Chuck/Coop said consolingly. "She got caught up in the moment." The look he gave Vi was repentant, as if he'd gotten caught up, too, and was interested in forgiveness.

"A pass? It's too soon for forgiveness all around." Violet curled her fingers into fists, not to slug Kelcie, but to keep from slugging Chuck/Coop. "Do you know how valuable that ring in her coat pocket is? My dad's going to kill both of us if we lose it."

"Not to mention, my heart will be broken," Grandma Dotty said, only half-seriously. She was still shooting dark looks Kelcie's way.

"Let's stop arguing and look for your coat." Without waiting for agreement, Chuck/Coop led the way into the house.

Violet hustled Grandma Dotty after him. But they were waylaid by Marguerite, who offered to loan Dotty and Kelcie dry clothes. While they were changing, Chuck, Coop and Vi searched the house and grounds, looking for Xuri and the coat thief. But the fashion designer and her black-wearing, modeling entourage appeared to have moved on. Grandma Dotty's coat was nowhere to be found.

"I looked everywhere," Chuck/Coop told Vi when he

bumped into her on the front steps. He was barefoot, holding his wet shoes and socks in one hand, still wearing his soaked slacks and shirt.

He hadn't needed to help Violet search. The wind off the ocean was probably chilling him to the bone in those wet clothes. The shirt clung to all those abs in a way that said, *Forgive me*. And...

Do not forgive him!

Violet forced her gaze up to his face, his dear, sweet face.

"I didn't find the guy who pushed me in the pool or the coat he took," Chuck/Coop was saying, confirming that the night was turning out to be a disaster. "You?"

"I can't find any of them," Vi admitted, trying unsuccessfully to find the anger over being lied to. "Thanks for looking."

Chuck/Coop smiled.

And for a moment, Violet almost smiled back. No matter who he'd introduced himself as, he was still nice. But then she remembered that he was a wealthy playboy who couldn't hold down an honest job. He was just another guy Harvard would frown upon. "We'll find our own way home." Vi turned to go back inside.

He caught her arm. "Please. Give me a chance, Vivi. Give us a chance."

Vivi.

Her heart melted a little more.

Simon joined them, also still in his wet clothes. "The dude is gone. I say we call the police."

"They'll never find him." Chuck/Coop shook his head. "Unlike Dotty, he won't wear that coat in the summer heat. Maybe the valet saw him get into a car. And maybe he's driving something that'll be easy to find." He glanced toward the driveway.

"My phone, Vi." Grandma Dotty came out the front door with Kelcie. They both wore black leggings and black tank tops.

"My phone's in the coat pocket along with my ring and that twenty."

Simon shook his head. "If we call your phone, they'll just shut it off and throw it away."

My phone...

"No," Violet said, understanding dawning. She scrambled to take her cell phone out of her little purse. "We have the *Find My Friends* app." The family used it sometimes to locate Grandma Dotty if she wandered off. She toggled to the app and selected her grandmother's phone as the location.

Five heads bent over her phone as the app zoomed in on a map.

"It's a house," Chuck/Coop said.

"It's not just any house." Kelcie grinned. "That's where the after party is being held, I bet."

"I'll order an Uber." Violet noted the address.

"Don't." Chuck/Coop placed a hand over her phone. He waved to the valet with his other hand. "We've got my car."

"We're not going anywhere with you." It pained Violet to say, but it was the smart decision to make. She put her arms around her grandmother's shoulders and started down the front steps.

"My car will be here quicker than any car you order on an app," Chuck/Coop pointed out. "And given how hard those models fought for the coat, you'll need some muscle."

Against Vi's better judgment, she agreed.

∼

"I'm the first person to talk bad about Coop," Simon said from the front seat of the Lincoln Town car as he drove to the next party.

Coop considered stopping and dragging his childhood friend out of the vehicle.

"Go right ahead." Vivi sat in the back sandwiched between

Dotty and Kelcie, both of whom were snoozing beneath blankets Coop had produced from the trunk. Her phone sat in Coop's cupholder with the map calling out directions in a man's British accent.

"I'm the first person to talk bad about Coop because..." Simon glanced at Coop, who gripped the steering wheel tighter, bracing himself for the worst. "...I am him."

"What a crock." Coop very nearly pulled over and slugged him.

"Which *him* are you referring to?" Vivi asked in a chilly voice. "Chuck? Coop? Or Charles Cooper Pearson?"

"The Third," Simon added, still being annoying. "I'm Radcliff Simon Marchand the Fourth." Simon half-turned in his seat, staring back at Vivi in a way that had jealousy rearing its head once more in Coop.

He'd never really experienced a green-eyed monster before, at least not when it came to a woman.

Green-eyed monster... Another Shakespeare term.

And since Vivi wasn't talking to Coop, what was the point of using Shakespearean terms?

"Growing up, I went to all the same exclusive, private schools that Coop did. We competed for everything, from sports to girls. My name alone got me entrance and credit at stores, country clubs, and car dealerships. My great-grandfather has an engineering wing dedicated to him at the university I attended in Houston. My father is a top donor there. It didn't matter that my grades were sub-par. They were happy to have another generation of Marchands on campus." He nudged Coop's shoulder. "Sound familiar."

Too much so. Coop nodded.

"In four hundred feet, turn right on *Arrr-cher* Street." The British man stumbled over what to Coop was a simple street name.

He slowed for the right turn on Archer.

"And then, my father died," Simon said quietly. "Right there at his desk. It made me realize I didn't want to work my fingers to the bone just to increase already unimaginable family fortunes. I had just started catching the bug for engineering and was competing with Coop for internships when my father died and—"

"You're an engineer?" Vivi asked Coop.

He nodded absently and just as absently said, "*Like madness is the glory of this life.*"

"Shakespeare? Now?" Vivi shook her head.

"Now is the perfect time for Shakespeare. We're in the midst of a crisis." Coop caught Vivi's eye in the rear view mirror.

She looked away.

"Anyway," Simon continued. "I loved electronic engineering because I loved solving problems and puzzles. But after Dad's funeral, I couldn't do it anymore. Who needs a faster superconductor anyway?"

"In one hundred feet, turn left on Bayview Drive," the Brit instructed.

Coop obeyed, still noodling over Simon's admission. Simon's life was on a parallel track of sorts to his.

The tell-tale signs of a party in progress were evident on the semi-rural street. Cars were parked on each shoulder, crammed together so tight there was no way they'd been left there by anyone other than a valet, paid to make the most use of space.

"What did you do, Simon?" Vivi asked with what sounded like sincere interest.

Mr. Green-Eyed Monster envied Simon for having broken through her guard. But he had no one to blame for her cold shoulder but himself.

"I drowned my grief and unhappiness in alcohol." Simon didn't sound repentant. In fact, he sounded rather cheerful. "As luck would have it, my efforts were made at a very trendy restaurant where the chef knew me and had a heart. Every time I showed up to drink, he'd take me back into the kitchen. Oh, he'd use some excuse about wanting to share a new, exclusive beverage with me. It wasn't long before I was showing up earlier and earlier, helping him prep food and participating in his food experiments as he searched for new ways to impress someone's palate."

"It was fate. And you found your gift," Coop muttered, a bit envious because he had yet to bring his to life. "All without having been cut off and ordered to pretend to be someone else."

"Is that what your father made you do?" At his nod, Simon swore. "That's messed up, man."

Vivi was noticeably silent.

Cars were lined up to enter the driveway of the massive estate.

Coop entered the que, sticking his head out the window and whistled shrilly, trying to catch the valet's attention.

"So, you see, Violet." Simon turned in his seat to face her. "Coop's situation may have been different. But we have more in common than either of you thinks."

Vivi made a noncommittal noise. "Why wouldn't your family support your interest in opening a restaurant? You've been looking for financing, right?"

Coop took note of that for later.

"My grandfather believes I don't respect him or my legacy," Simon said. "If I did, as the oldest, I'd move into the office where my father died and take on his duties. My kid sister would love that office and the work. She's a business management major at Baylor. And since she wants the role, I want her to have it. But sometimes, the life you choose and the way you feel life should be... Well, you have to go it alone."

Those last words played on repeat in Coop's head: *you have to go it alone.* How true those words felt.

Vivi leaned over the seat and grabbed her phone from the cupholder. "The coat is here."

The valet gave them a ticket for the car. Coop tipped him big and instructed him to keep the Town Car close. He didn't antici-pate being at the party long. It wouldn't be hard to spot Dotty's big white jacket. And given the people they were dealing with, they'd probably want to make a quick exit.

Meanwhile, Vivi roused Dotty and Simon roused Kelcie, and then they all headed into the house for another loud, packed party.

A live band played somewhere. But the acoustics were bad, and Coop didn't recognize the song for all the heavy *boom-boom-da-boom.*

They reached the front door. Coop peered over the heads of people sardined in front of him. "Oh, no."

"Do you see it?" Vivi demanded from the step below him.

"Is the thief inside?" Dotty asked, bouncing up and down on her toes.

"The coat had kittens." Coop spotted several people wearing jackets exactly like Dotty's. "I see at least thirty people wearing them." It made no sense. It had to be stifling in that packed house.

"Fifty," Simon added, frowning. "They're outside on the back patio, too."

"How are we going to figure out which coat is Dotty's?" Vivi groaned. "My dot in the app only indicates the jacket is at this house, not exactly where."

"We're going to get close to every person wearing a coat as if we have seduction in mind." Dotty shimmied her shoulders. "And then we're going to slip our hands inside their jacket." She extended her arms, as if frisking a suspect. "And grab onto what's mine."

"And get arrested for groping a stranger?" Coop shook his head.

But Dotty was already burrowing her way through the crowd, followed by Kelcie. They were two peas in a trouble-seeking pod.

"This is going to turn ugly real quick," Simon said before diving into the crush. He wasn't going to lose Dotty this time.

"Hey, the coats each have a different design on the back." Vivi tugged on the back of Coop's shirt. "Grandma Dotty's has blue bunnies."

"That's good to know." Coop turned to face her, inching aside to let Simon and Kelcie go past. "Can we talk later? About...us?"

She shrugged, a guarded expression on her face. "If we don't get arrested, sure."

Chapter Eleven

THE PRESS OF BODIES WAS LIKE BEING ON THE SUBWAY after a packed house at Madison Square Garden.

And I used to like this kind of thing.

Violet used to like Chuck, too. Until she found out he was someone else. Now, she didn't know how she felt about him. He'd kissed her while pretending to be someone—*something*—else entirely.

Violet recognized someone from Kelcie's boot camp classes. She touched her arm, smiling. "Hey, what's with all the coats." She pointed to a woman wearing a big, white coat with a blue cat printed on the back.

The boot camp woman leaned closer, shouting in Vi's ear, "Xuri's doing a social media event." She pointed toward a man standing on the stairwell filming with a big, professional-sized camera that made Violet cringe inside. And then she pointed in the opposite direction. "She's giving out coats in the kitchen if there are any left. It's too hot for me."

Violet made her way to the kitchen, passing groups of people with drinks in their hands who were shouting conversations with each other.

"The sailing was perfect today!" a man said as she bumped his shoulder.

Sailboats only reminded Violet of being with Coop and talking about Shakespeare as sailboats dotted the ocean's horizon.

A rail thin college-age girl wearing one of Xuri's coats nearly collided with Violet as she went the other way.

Vi grabbed hold of her jacket as she squeezed by, only releasing it when she realized a puppy was painted on the back, not bunnies. "Sorry!" She ignored the girl's dirty look and pressed on.

"The salmon at Fabrizi's is to die for!" a woman in a crop top and skimpy skirt shouted to her cluster of people.

Violet wasn't a huge fan of salmon. She had a sweet tooth. And since she was a homebody, having a handsome man deliver her frozen yogurt on a warm, moonlit night was about as close to perfect as things got.

Not that I'm going to forgive him...am I?

She didn't know.

A shirtless, buff young man strutted out from a hallway into Vi's path. He wore a big white jacket, but he'd flung the sides of the jacket behind him. In order to check the back, she paused to let him pass.

A blue bird.

"Rats." Vi soldiered on.

"My Ferrari has never given me problems! I'd trade your Tesla in!"

She dodged the small group of men posturing about their fancy cars. All this shouting just to be heard. The jumble of music and noise rang in her ears until all she could distinguish was the beat of the bass and the drum.

Why did anyone consider this fun?

Finally, she squeezed her way into the kitchen. A very skinny, short woman held court in front of a bright red, ten burner gas stove as if she had a coveted purpose in this drama. She leaned on a stack of coats on the kitchen counter.

A. Stack. Of. Coats.

There had to be ten, maybe more.

Violet hurried forward and grabbed a coat, intending to rummage through the stack, looking for blue bunnies.

"Are you participating?" The self-important woman wore goth-like make-up and had a widow's peak, making her look vampirish. She arm-barred Vi away from the coats. She had skinny arms, but they were strong skinny arms.

"Participating? I'm looking for a coat that—"

"The coats are right here." The vampirish woman handed Violet a jacket. It had a blue llama painted on the back. "You have to wear the coat and your dance moves have to pass muster with Xuri if you want to get on the yacht."

"I'm sorry? What yacht?"

"For the after-after party." Vampira rolled her eyes.

"Hey, you found it?" Simon reached for the jacket Violet held. "Wait. Why are there so many?"

Kelcie appeared at his elbow. "Oh. My. Gosh. Are they free? Can I have one?"

"You have to dance for it, peasants," Vampira said with another eye roll. "No one is supposed to be here who doesn't know the rules. You can't get to the next party without Xuri's blessing. And you can't get to the next party if Xuri doesn't approve of your dancing and let you on the yacht."

"How do we get on the boat exactly?" Simon asked.

"How else?" Vampira said sharply. "By dancing down the runway in a coat. Do you want a coat or not?"

Violet grabbed two more coats for Grandma Dotty and Coop. Simon and Kelcie each grabbed one. Despite there not being blue bunnies on the back, they each dug into the interior pockets. No ring, no twenty dollar bill, no cell phone.

"Layla! It's time!" someone called from the living room.

"Don't disappoint me, peasants," Layla/Vampira said gravely before strutting like a model out the door.

They followed Vampira—Violet wasn't ready to think of her

as Layla yet—out of the kitchen and joined the stream of party goers heading toward the private boat dock. The cameraman had moved to a nearby rise in the garden and was aiming his lens at the crowd.

Vi ducked her head.

Ahead of her, Coop—he was no longer Chuck—was standing with Grandma Dotty. "Did you realize this is a dance-off?"

"And I don't have my coat." Grandma Dotty's gaze lit on the coats in Violet's arms. "Is that mine?"

"It's a loaner until we find yours." Violet handed her grandmother and Coop their jackets before putting hers on. "We're not letting that thief get away with this." Not that Vi planned on participating in the dance off. She was just going to blend in.

"Look! Our thief is on the boat deck." Coop pointed out the man dancing on the upper deck of the luxury yacht. He wore a white coat, but his back faced the sea. "How did he get on first? The competition hasn't started."

"Isn't it obvious by his hollow cheeks and black outfit?" Simon scoffed. "He's one of Xuri's models."

And he was onboard. Gah! Vi's spirits plummeted. Now it was imperative that she get on that yacht. The likelihood of her doing so *and* remaining anonymous was very slim. In fact, the chances of her being identified was much more likely than her passing Xuri's dance test.

A pair of very young, very pretty, very talented dancers wearing the requisite white denim jackets pranced down the dock toward the yacht where Xuri stood at the foot of the gang plank.

The fashion designer had changed out of her be-ribboned dress and into a black cat suit. Gone were the big platform shoes. She wore bright red pumps.

The dancers reached Xuri, circling her as they executed what to Vi seemed like professional moves.

But Xuri shook her head.

Vampira struck a gong.

And then two big bouncers blocked the dancers from the

gangplank. They advanced, grabbing the two women and tossing them off the dock.

The women screamed. And then they laughed, having landed on an inflatable raft.

One of the muscled security guards untied their mooring and let the tide to carry them to shore. They had no oars. But that didn't seem to bother them.

"This is barbaric." And since it was being videoed, that meant it would get tons of views. Vi groaned, not wanting to be caught on camera or thrown off the dock. "We can't get on the boat without dancing to Xuri's satisfaction. There's no way anyone but Kelcie is getting on that boat."

"Are you saying I can't dance?" Simon grinned. "Honey, I can dance." He slipped on his coat and took Kelcie by the arm. "We've got this."

"I've got this, too." Her grandmother strutted down the path.

The gong sounded again. Another couple was pushed onto one of the inflatable rafts and cast to sea. The boat carrying the first pair of dismissed dancers was nearly to shore.

"Do you dance?" Violet asked Coop, biting her bottom lip.

"I'm from Texas." He tugged the lapels of his white denim jacket, which somehow didn't look ridiculous on him. "I can two-step. You?"

"I think I've proven all week that I can't hip hop. And I need to protect my identity." Violet's shoulders tensed. Was that even possible? "But if you put your arms around me and I put my hood up, I can follow your lead in the two-step."

As if an omen, another gong sounded.

～

As usual, Dotty had muscled her way to the head of the line.

Hood up, she looked small, like a little kid wearing her dad's snow jacket.

"What happens if Dotty gets on the boat, and we don't?"

Coop wasn't optimistic about their chances. And he wanted to try and shelter Vivi from being featured in Xuri's social media campaign. He'd bet the designer wasn't above name-dropping.

The gong was sounding more often than not. Dancers were tossed to rafts with alarming frequency.

Xuri must have anticipated this because there were at least twenty rafts tied to either side of the dock. But Dotty needed a protector. The jacket thief had already proven his desperation to get a coat. What would he do to keep it?

"There's no telling what your grandmother will do if she gets her hands on that guy," Coop said to Vivi, shrugging into his white, puffy jacket, which was surprisingly warm given his still-damp clothes. Simon and Kelcie had already made their way down to the dock.

"Doom and gloom much?" Hood up, Vivi shook out her arms and then rolled her head from side-to-side, bouncing on her toes—all of which Coop assumed was her warming up to dance. "Here's a worst-case scenario for you. What happens if *none* of us get on the boat?"

"We can still find the jacket with your cell phone." Watching the coat thief dance happily on the upper deck, Coop frowned. The jerk. Did he have to look so happy?

"Sure, we can find her phone." Vivi didn't sound as optimistic as her words. "We'll find it as long as my grandmother's battery stays charged and there's cell phone reception. I have no idea where that yacht's sailing. If it's out to sea..."

"Hey, there are five of us. Those are good odds." Coop stared at Vivi. Despite all the drama and escapades of the evening, she still looked gorgeous. Wind-blown, worried, but gorgeous. "We'll get your grandmother's ring back. I promise."

"You can't promise when something's out of your control." Vivi gasped, grasping his arm, giving him hope for their future once this night was over and they had time to talk. "It's Grandma Dotty's turn."

On the dock, Dotty shoved her coat sleeves to her elbows and then went to work. She twerked. She banged her arms and bobbed her head as she covered several feet of dock. She worked the jacket back and forth across her back as if it was a towel and she'd just gotten out of the shower. She bent over and walked toward Xuri, arms swinging like an elephant's trunk.

"Wow." Coop was impressed. "Did Kelcie teach her those moves this week? She's not bad."

"Yeah. Once Grandma Dotty sets her mind to something..." The old lady spun, nearly falling in the ocean.

The crowd gasped. So did Vivi.

And then everyone cheered when Dotty recovered and shimmied her way to Xuri.

No gong.

"She made it." Vivi shook Coop's arm. "What am I going to do? I should have tried harder to learn the routines in class."

Dotty hugged Xuri, turned to the remaining crowd and shot her hands in the air as if she'd just scored the winning goal, and then she spun around and strutted up the gangplank, working the jacket like any good model would.

Coop was suddenly struck by a thought. "What's the likelihood Dotty forgets about the coat thief once she's on board?"

"Fifty-fifty." Vivi let go of him and wrung her hands. "It depends on how hungry she is and how distracting the other passengers are."

"Squirrel," Coop murmured, nodding.

Dotty took something from a tray a waiter was holding. She ate it at the rail, apparently ready to watch the rest of the competitors instead of finding the coat thief and her anniversary ring. Coop thought that was a good thing.

Guests who hadn't passed the test stumbled out of the inflatable boats at the shoreline. A few flunkies towed the rubber life rafts up the beach so they wouldn't be taken back out to sea.

"This is quite the production," Coop noted.

"That's why Xuri's fashions are so popular. She's a spectacle." Vivi tossed a few jabs in the air, shadow boxing.

"Hey, Rocky." Coop claimed her hands. "We're dancing, not getting into the ring."

"You don't know how this will end." Her words had multiple meanings—the dance-off, the ring recovery effort, their fledgling romance.

"I know how one thing will end," he told her, kissing her knuckles. "We're each other's fate."

Before he could tell her about a decade's old kissing test, Kelcie and Simon stepped onto the dock and started dancing. Kelcie was a beast, really hitting all the high notes in whatever moves she was making. Meanwhile, Simon did the Dad Dance behind her, moving as if he were just a backdrop to highlight Kelcie's talent.

Whatever they did worked. They made it on the boat.

"I feel better now," Vivi told Coop, gazing at him from under the faux fur trim of her hood. "Hopefully, Simon can find my grandmother's things."

"I'll feel better when we walk up that gang plank."

Several other dancers didn't make the cut. Gong-gong-gong-gong.

They tumbled into the life rafts without seeming to be too upset at losing. The beach was now littered with rafts and the carefully groomed grounds above the beach were dotted with rejected dancers and other hangers-on, all waiting for a grand finale. Whatever that was.

Soon, it was their turn.

"Hoods up." Vivi flipped Coop's hood in place. "We need attitude to make the cut."

"Follow my lead." Impulsively, Coop planted a kiss on Vivi's nose.

"Shakespeare," she warned.

He didn't wait to hear more. He launched them into the two-step.

It wasn't a popular choice.

They were booed.

A quick glance toward the yacht revealed the coat thief as a chief boo-er.

Grrr.

Coop kept on dancing, leading Vivi toward their destination.

A gong sounded, reverberating over the boos.

"*No!*" Vivi cried as a bouncer tried to take her by her shoulders. She ducked under his arms and started dancing on her own, presumably using some of those moves she'd learned in hip hop cardio.

Coop had no time to watch. What felt like a Mack truck rammed into Coop and sent him flying through the air. He landed on a bobbing life raft and was pelted by the rope that set him free.

～

VIOLET WASN'T LETTING that boat sail without her. She didn't care if she made Xuri's highlight reel. Her grandmother needed her.

Which meant Vi didn't look back to see if Coop was okay, even though she wanted to. She'd seen him tackled and tossed off the dock. She had to believe he was fine.

She channeled her grandmother's enthusiasm for dance and boogied her way toward Xuri, working all the dance moves she could remember from class into her forward progress.

Xuri stood at the end of the dock, her expression shadowed by her dark, dramatic make-up and the ship lights above her. But Vi could tell Xuri watched her dance with gong-ringing on her mind. There was a tick to Xuri's otherwise expressionless face.

Fear knotted in Vi's gut, threatening to spread and stiffen her limbs. Darn it. She needed her body to be fluid in its starts and stops, in her hip sways and shoulder thrusts. But fear built. The fear that she wasn't going to be allowed on board. The fear that she couldn't protect her grandmother even if she did receive passage.

The fear layered inside of her like a stack of dry wood for a bonfire, just waiting for a match to go up in flames. It built and expanded and then... The fear morphed. The fear... The fear made Violet mad.

Mad that this evening hadn't been going her way. Angry that she'd kissed a man who hadn't told her his real name. Furious that the safety of her grandmother came down to a dancing exhibition. Fuming that a designer was slowly turning to the gong-holder.

She glared at Xuri and screamed as she zombie-walked forward, working her stiff arms up-and-down to the beat of the music. She stopped mere inches from Xuri and that cold, regal face. She stopped screaming, too. But her mouth...

Her mouth kept moving and her hands fisted at her sides as she cried, *"I'm. Getting on. This yacht."*

Chapter Twelve

"WHAT DO YOU MEAN I CAN'T DANCE AGAIN?" COOP tried to push his way past Xuri's tiny assistant to the dock where Vivi and the last of the dancers had been taken aboard, escorted by Xuri. Two parties tonight. And two dunkings. His flimsy inflatable raft had been taken out by a wave cresting mere feet from shore. His cell phone was certainly dead. His shoes were soaked, feet squishing in them. "I want a do-over."

"You had your turn. You were rejected. You lose." Xuri's tiny, militant assistant took too much pleasure in those words.

The yacht engines came to life, rumbling loud enough to almost cover the gangplank banging, preparing to be stowed.

Were they waiting for this woman? The bouncers were already on board, along with the cameraman.

Coop glanced at his one roadblock.

I can take her. I can toss her into a life raft.

The cameraman was at the railing on the top deck, aiming at the shore.

Coop's jaw jutted forward. Making a spectacle of himself on film wouldn't help Vivi. He drew a deep breath. "My people are on that boat." Coop pointed at the yacht. *My women.* "They need me." *Vivi needs me.*

Xuri's assistant shook her head. "Your girl didn't need you when she danced her way into the after-after party." She pointed at dry land. "Stay, loser." And then she turned and hurried to get on board the yacht before it set sail.

Coop stood alone on the dock. The other rejected party-goers were leaving, working their way back to the house and, presumably, their rides home.

He couldn't see Vivi. Or Dotty. Or Kelcie. Or...

There.

Simon separated himself from the crowd on the upper deck next to the coat thief. Words were exchanged. Or at least, their mouths worked. He was too far away to hear over the engine churning. Arms were flung about. Hands connected with shoulders. The thief shoved Simon. Simon shoved the thief. And then there was a scuffle as the yacht pulled away from the dock and...

Simon fell overboard, creating a big splash.

The yacht continued to pull away. No one seemed to care that a man with poor swimming skills was being left behind.

Coop walked down to the shoreline, keeping an eye on his friend in case he needed to jump in and rescue him.

Simon finally made it to shore, dragging the coat behind him. "That's it. I'm done." He flung the coat in an empty, beached life raft.

"But...we have to find them."

"You can find them, Coop. I have to cater a brunch tomorrow. Those women leave a trail of chaos in their wake." He stomped toward the house. Or he would have stomped if he'd sloshed less.

Coop stayed where he was, watching the yacht sail out to sea.

It wasn't chaos the Summer women left in their wake. It was his heart. Vivi and Dotty had somehow managed to find a place in it this past week.

Dotty with her unexpected charm and zest for life. Vivi with her deep intellect, thoughtfulness, and soft heart. Vivi with the big brown eyes he could get lost in, the hair that teased his senses for a touch, the one person he wanted to be with from the moment his eyes opened to the moment he drifted off to sleep.

The one person.

His person.

"I love Vivi," he said in quiet wonder. Not that anyone was around to hear. He'd never been in love as an adult. He'd dated. Drifted in and out of relationships.

"Hey!" Simon called from behind him. "The caterer has a team out at an estate up the coast. I have the address of where the yacht is going."

The boat was just a small dot of light on the water.

Coop turned and ran up the hill. "Where?"

Squish. Squish. Squish.

It felt like he was trudging through mud in his wet, salty clothes. Coop didn't care. He was going to be there for Vivi when the boat docked.

Instead of telling him where they were going, Simon ran toward the house, his wet slacks practically falling off. "Come on. Let's go."

Coop knew he should be grateful to Simon for the information. It was just...now he wouldn't have his people all to himself. "What happened to you being done with *those women.*"

Simon hitched up his pants without breaking stride. "I can't let Kelcie down. She's liable to try something foolish like I did."

The house was empty except for the cleaning crew.

"Kelcie?" Not Vivi? Coop ran faster, catching up to his former friend.

"Yeah. When I said those women, I meant Kelcie and Dotty. They're a lot alike." He gave a mirthless laugh. "Don't you remember my type? Blond. Unpredictable. Always ready for an adventure."

"Yeah." Coop remembered now. "And my type was..."

"Any woman."

"Well, it's Vivi now." And hopefully forever. "How'd that coat thief get the best of you?"

"He got lucky." Simon wrung out his shirt, leaving his own wake on the white marble floor. "I stumbled over something. He just used the momentum to send me over the rail."

"A likely story." Coop grinned.

They reached the front porch. A valet took their claim ticket and read the numbers into a walkie-talkie. And then the two men fell silent.

"You think they'll be okay?" Coop asked, worried once more.

"Sure. Maybe. I hope so." Simon shrugged. "Violet seems to have a good head on her shoulders."

Violet, who'd been warming up to dance by shadow-boxing.

Coop ran a few steps down the driveway toward the approaching valet. "Where's my car?"

∿

"MISS SUMMER. I must talk to you." Xuri spoke with the haughty tone of royalty on the outer deck of the yacht as they headed out to sea. She snapped her fingers at Vampira. "Layla, bring my coat."

And Violet, who'd seen Simon fall overboard, knew to tread carefully with her host.

"Such anger when you dance." Xuri's gaze stroked Violet up-and-down in an unwelcome assessment. "Where did it come from?"

"My grandmother—"

"Ah." Xuri batted away Violet's answer with a swipe of her hand through the air. "You are the boring Summer. Everyone knows this."

Boring.

It was one thing to regulate her life to Harvard standards, and another to have her lifestyle tossed back in her face. Ten years ago, no one would have called Vi boring or would have been surprised that she'd entered a dance off.

The frustration that had driven Vi on the dock resurfaced.

"I'm not boring. I'm serious about my career goals. Do you know how hard I worked to get a position at Harvard? Or how hard I'm working to be awarded tenure?"

"Yes. I do." Xuri seemed serious. "To be the best... In the best of places or industries... It is hard." Xuri's expression almost turned...empathetic. And in that moment, it felt like Xuri and Violet connected, until the fashion designer added, "But *I'm* not boring." And then she gave Vi a superior smile.

Shades of every bully Vi had ever encountered in school. And those shades...they struck all the discordant, angry places inside of her.

"You can have your fun." Violet drew herself up and rolled her shoulders back. "You may not be boring, but I'm not a shallow, attention-seeking woman who'll do anything for a trending hashtag. And for that, I'm glad." *That's right. Boo-yah!* "If you'll excuse me, I have to locate my grandmother."

Violet found Grandma Dotty and Kelcie on the upper deck. Heads together, they were watching the coat thief across the way. Pop music played, but softly, the quietest music had been played all night.

Vi joined the pair. "Why don't you just go up and ask him for your phone and ring back?" But instead of taking her own advice, Violet took a glass of champagne from a passing waiter. She needed the anger with the world to recede or she might do something rash, something unbecoming of a Harvard professor.

She frowned at the cameraman filming the gathering and tossed up her coat hood.

"We have to be careful. That guy is ruthless," Kelcie said in awe. "He threw Simon overboard."

"Or maybe Simon didn't ask nicely." Vi sipped her champagne. It was cheap, just like Xuri's promotional stunt.

The coat thief was facing their way, dancing with a group of friends. Or rather, they were holding drinks like props in a mannequin's hand and doing a side-to-side mom dance. None of the group had been forced to dance their way on board. Did they even have dance moves?

The anger inside of Vi refused to recede.

"I didn't hear Simon say please." Grandma Dotty had a glazed look about her, which she sometimes got when she was overly-tired. She needed rest and hydration.

But first things first. The coat and the ring had to be reclaimed.

"I'll handle it." Violet drained the champagne glass, hoping the alcohol would take effect soon since she still felt like she was one small thread away from attempting to throw someone overboard.

Calm down, Professor Summer.

Vi scoffed. The time for formalities and protocols had long passed. She crossed the deck toward the group of dancing models. She moved through the crowd like a killer shark with a familiar, ominous theme song playing in her head.

Da-da. Da-da. Da-da, da-da, da-da.

Jaws.

On some level, she knew she should back up, turn around, and cool off. But on another level, she'd spent six years being the hard-working, trouble-free Violet. If ever there was a time to let the old Violet loose, it was now.

And so, she walked past the cameraman, never taking her eyes off her target. And when the male model finally glanced up and met her gaze, she tossed her head to acknowledge that *yeah, I'm looking at you, loser.*

He smiled at her. A friendly smile.

Only then did the ocean breeze hitting her face find a chink in her wrath.

I need to be adult about this. Classy. Composed.

Violet slowed.

The coat thief met her halfway. He had a slight build and finely chiseled features. He carried himself well in Xuri's jacket.

His mother probably loved him. She probably bragged about him during Bunco nights and at the beauty salon.

Vi drew a deep breath, drawing on the poise of Professor Violet Summer.

"Hey." The young model greeted Vi with the same superiority Xuri looked down on people. But he was no Xuri. He wasn't even an ancient professor dressing down a young, associate professor for behavior unbecoming a representative of Harvard University.

"Hey," Violet said, feeling twitchy.

He sipped a dark drink from a tumbler, most likely Rum & Coke because he didn't know any better. "I like how you ditched your date."

Shakespeare.

The anger bubbled in her veins once more.

"I hear they have beds downstairs." He smiled, running his palms over his chest and his eyes over her. "I like older women."

Older women? Rage!

"Hey, baby." Vi couldn't stop herself any longer, despite seeing the cameraman move closer out of the corner of her eye. She grabbed hold of the young stud's coat lapels with both hands. "I'm not smiling at you because I want to see what's in your diaper, chisel cheeks. I have had a really bad day."

Harvard, Vi. Think of Harvard.

"Ah." His smile grew. He touched a lock of her hair resting on the shoulder of her jacket. "A bad hair day?"

Rage!

It was far too late for taking the high road. Lines had been crossed. This punk thought he was entitled to treat others poorly, just because he was pretty and had caught Xuri's eye. He had to be taught a lesson.

"Good looks and thick hair fade fast as you age, jerk." Violet dragged him closer by those coat lapels. "I don't care about your ego. If you don't show me what's in your inner coat pocket right now, I'm going to make a very loud joke about how bad you were in the sack at the first party of the night. And I'm going to continue to make performance jokes at your expense until your underage, underwear model friends believe me."

"Why would you do that?" he squeaked, mousy nature revealed.

"Because you have no manners and no soul. You stole this jacket from a little old lady. And your mother would *not* be proud."

"I..." Instead of arguing, he opened his lapels and let Vi rummage through those inner pockets.

"They're empty." Violet checked a second time. "Did you spend the twenty and throw the cell phone and ring away?" Vi's knees weakened, along with her anger. She'd been so certain her grandmother had told the truth about putting her things in the coat pocket. But they could be anywhere.

The cameraman moved nearer, more a shark than Vi had ever been.

"I don't know what you're talking about." The young model jerked away. And then he composed himself, blew her a kiss, and scurried back to his friends.

Violet stared at him blankly for several seconds until something registered.

There weren't blue bunnies on the back of his jacket.

~

"I KNOW THIS ADDRESS." Coop turned down a too familiar driveway. "The after-after party is at my family's house. It's time to call the cops."

"Why?" Simon had been huddling in front of the heating vents. He leaned back to look at Coop.

"This is my family's vacation home." For the first time since picking up Vivi and Dotty this evening, Coop felt as if he was in control. And for a breath or two, he forgot how cold and wet he was. Not even a thirty minute drive could dry his clothes and even if it could have, salt from the ocean dunking made them stiff and sticky. "If this is where Xuri's party boat is heading, I'm going to get her arrested for trespassing."

"That might not be such a good idea. You do know that every property in the Hamptons is for rent, right?" Simon returned to his position making love to the heating vents, stretching the placate of his polo shirt to allow hot air inside. "I can't count the number of times my old man rented out our property. You can get five or six figures a night. With money like that, you don't need to pay the mortgage."

"Can you see my dad renting out his home?" Not only couldn't he imagine it, but Coop had never heard his father mention letting their house out.

"I'd bet good money he's doing just that." Simon adjusted his heating vents. "You think Xuri owns that yacht? Think again. The luxury life is absolutely for sale or rent by wannabees. And the smart wealthy take advantage of that fact."

"Still..."

"Even if your father wouldn't rent your *house*, he could rent the beach access and dock." Simon sounded convincing. "You see those catering trucks? That's proof that something is going on."

"And I was looking forward to seeing Xuri taken away in handcuffs." Coop parked the Town Car near the front door. "On the bright side, I have dry clothes upstairs."

"Good. I wasn't looking forward to working in these clothes. Simon paused, hand on the door handle. "What about a key?"

That he didn't have. His parents had a set, as did the housekeeper, he supposed.

The two men got out of the car. This side of the house was sheltered from the wind.

Coop glanced at the second story windows, wondering if any were open and if he could scale the façade if they were.

Simon was already halfway to the side yard. "Come on. The caterers are around back and they're expecting me. Maybe they have a spare shirt or two."

Light from inside the house caught Coop's eye. "They're in

the kitchen. That means we can get in the house. Follow my lead. I'll introduce myself and say I startled you. And because you lack cat-like grace, you fell into the pool. You do have a habit of tumbling into water."

"I wouldn't joke," Simon teased. "Or I'll throw *you* in the pool this time."

"You wish." Coop laughed. It felt good, like the first real laugh of the night.

Maybe things were looking up, after all.

⁓

TOGETHER, Violet, Kelcie, and Grandma Dotty searched the boat for the jacket with blue bunnies on the back.

They started on the top deck and worked their way down to the private salon behind the bridge, followed by the inquisitive cameraman. Since they'd been barred from going into the bedrooms below decks, this was the end of the line.

The three stopped to regroup, staring at the one coat they hadn't examined—the one Xuri wore.

"It can't be her," Grandma Dotty whispered.

"How would she get the coat in the first place?" Kelcie asked.

"There's only one way to find out." Violet approached Xuri, who sat on a chair that resembled a thrown and was encircled by minions dressed in black, no white coats. Vi gave her host a cold stare and colder greeting, "Xuri."

Grandma Dotty came to stand beside Vi.

Xuri arched her brows, waiting to hear why they were demanding an audience.

But this time when Xuri stared at her, words failed Vi. She felt no anger, no indignation, no urgent need to find her grandmother. And lacking that spark, Violet was much too aware that every word she said was being recorded. College professors, especially those from Ivy League schools, didn't make desperate demands of cutting-edge celebrities or put themselves in positions of vulnerability with said celebs. Not on camera. And certainly not when they were up for tenure.

Vi considered turning around and leaving, tail between her legs. She'd have lost her grandmother's valuable anniversary ring, but she'd have managed to keep Grandma Dotty and Vi's reputation safe...assuming the cameraman hadn't recorded her dance audition on the dock.

Maybe it was best to retreat and fight another day. She could file a police report or something.

The corner of Xuri's mouth twitched. And then her smile broadened as if she considered this battle of wills already won.

Fire sparked in Violet's belly. A spark, not a flame.

Seize the day. That was Coop's voice in her head, quoting a Latin phrase Shakespeare had used in a play. And surprisingly, his voice came to her without any of the anger and disappointment she'd felt when thinking of him over the past few days. She didn't care that he'd been fired. She understood why he'd presented himself as Chuck, not Coop. But Charles Cooper Pearson the Third... He would never retreat when something he wanted was so near. Never.

And she wouldn't either.

"Why did you give my grandmother that coat and then steal it back?" Violet moved to Xuri's side, edging out one of her entourage, and gave the sleeve of white denim coat the designer was wearing a little tug. "She would have returned it if you'd asked for it."

Grandma Dotty's mouth dropped open. "So it's true? That's my coat?"

Xuri smiled warmly at her grandmother, avoiding Violet altogether. "This coat was the first I made. Layla should not have sent it to you."

That was no apology. A bit more of Violet's nerve returned, but before she could say anything more, her grandmother spoke.

"I understand why you love that coat. It has sentimental value to me, too, although not for the same reasons." Grandma Dotty came to stand on the other side of Xuri's chair, easily squirming between Xuri and Vampira. "My wedding ring is in one of the jacket pockets. If you hand it over, along with my emergency money and my cell phone, I won't arm wrestle you for it."

Xuri chuckled.

"I wouldn't laugh," Vi said tightly. "She'll do it. You know, she will."

Xuri's good humor evaporated.

"I know I'm just an old lady with a bucket list," Grandma Dotty continued somberly, looking wrung out but surprisingly clear of mind. "But I believed you really wanted to do something different, to make a statement that your fashions are for everybody, and that you design for attitude not age."

Vi glanced at the cameraman. He was adjusting his lens, as if zooming in for a close-up.

Xuri was frowning. "Ask anyone and they will tell you. My designs are different."

"But you're not brave enough to do something *age* different," Violet said in a low, hard voice. "And you're not brave enough to tell my grandmother you gave her the wrong jacket." Violet slipped out of her jacket and let it drop to the deck. "I refuse to wear anything made by a coward."

Kelcie and Grandma Dotty shrugged out of their coats, making a show of discarding them on the floor.

Xuri's gaze darted from the rejected jackets to the cameraman and then to Vi.

Slowly, she reached inside her jacket's inner pocket. She handed over Grandma Dotty's cell phone, a twenty dollar bill, and a large, sparkling diamond ring.

But she didn't apologize.

And for that, Violet would never forgive her.

Chapter Thirteen

Coop was waiting on the dock when the yacht arrived for the after-after party.

Coop. Violet could hardly believe it. She was so happy to see him, she waved.

She, Grandma Dotty, and Kelcie were the first ones off the yacht when the gang plank was secure. Without jackets, they were chilled to the bone.

Violet ran toward Coop. "How are you here?"

Coop swept her into his arms. "You're all safe?"

"Yes," Grandma Dotty came to stand next to them. "Thanks to Vi."

Violet wasn't going to take credit for anything. She'd lost her temper and nearly blown everything. She clung to Coop because his embrace was the first place she'd felt safe all night. "I'm so glad you found us."

"Me, too," he whispered in her ear.

"Violet got Dotty's stuff back," Kelcie told Coop, joining them on the dock. "She put Xuri in her place. It was awesome."

That also felt like an overstatement.

"I bet she was a sight to behold." Coop set Violet at arm's length and brushed her hair out of her eyes, peering at her like a doctor during an exam where he was unsure of the diagnosis. "I should have known you'd come out on top. Was Shakespeare quoted?"

"I was too angry for Shakespeare, although I did hear you quote him in my head." Not wanting to discuss the events of the boat ride while others were disembarking, Vi took Coop's hand and led the group toward shore. "How did you find us?"

"Simon gets all the credit." Coop glanced at Kelcie. "He was worried sick about all of you, but especially you, Kelcie."

"Me?" The petite fitness instructor fiddled with her hair as they transitioned to dry land.

"Yeah," Coop reassured her. "He's up cooking with the caterers. But he'd love to see you."

Kelcie hesitated, finger-combing her hair.

"Go on." Grandma Dotty nudged Kelcie forward. "Love doesn't care what you look like."

"Ain't that the truth." Coop stared at Vi with none of his usual playboy charm. No. This expression was more serious, much more so. "You ladies have never looked better to me."

Same.

Kelcie giggled and ran up the bank toward the house.

"I'm going to follow the scent of food." Grandma Dotty placed her hands on Vi's cheeks. "Take your time, dear."

"Are you sure?" Violet glanced down at her hand in Coop's. "Coop and I have a lot to discuss."

"I'm sure," Grandma Dotty said, glancing toward the house. "I see they've put blankets on the chairs. And look, Simon is waving me over." She returned his greeting, diamond ring catching the light. And then, she headed toward him and Kelcie.

Violet faced Coop, sighing because the worst of the night was over, and she hoped the best was about to begin.

But instead of kissing her or talking, Coop tugged her deeper into the grounds and away from the debarking party goers. "There's a covered look-out this way."

Violet was grateful to get away from all the posers. "All right, but just for a little bit. I can't let Grandma Dotty get into any more trouble."

And even though Vi was full of questions, she let Coop lead her to a three-sided windowed structure on a small bluff overlooking the ocean. Moonlight reflected on the water. The stars glimmered in the sky, clear and bright.

"You must be cold without that big white coat." Coop removed the jacket he was wearing and draped it over her shoulders. And then he drew her into the shelter of his arms. "I'm not sorry to see that puffy white coat go."

"Me, either."

They stood without talking, staring out at the spectacular view.

Vi leaned into him, soaking in his warmth and trying not to think about anything that had happened this evening or that could have happened. But one concern needed to be said. "Xuri filmed everything. My standing at Harvard—"

"Will be secured," Coop assured her in a confident voice. "You didn't sign a release, so they can't use that footage. My lawyer will make sure of it."

Reassured, Vi snuggled closer.

"You've been working all week on a book about Shakespeare," Coop said softly.

"And struggled on the chapter about fate." She lifted her head, giving it a little shake. "I think because Shakespeare was a firm believer in it and I'm not."

"Are you sure?" He drew back a little, stroking his fingers beneath her chin. "Our meeting has been rife with fate."

"Or coincidence," she pointed out.

"I can prove fate keeps intervening and that we're fated to be together," Coop said in a solemn voice that contrasted sharply against the music and laughter drifting to them from the house.

"Proof." Violet couldn't believe it. Not that she didn't want him to prove it. She did. Oh, how she did. But she knew there was no proof to be found. "You think we're each other's fate because we met on a beach?"

"Partly." He nodded. "Don't forget that I was hired to drive you around town."

"That's not enough. And even if it was—"

He kissed her.

It was a gentle kiss, accepting of nights spent in, of comfy clothes put on to roam about the house, of textbooks and dusty volumes sharing bed space. All of which was silly. It was her fantasy, not his.

He ended the kiss slowly. "We've met before. A long time ago. You may not remember but it was here in the Hamptons. I hung out at the gelato place a lot that summer. You know the one I'm talking about, don't you?" At her nod, he continued. "And one of your sisters sent you over to me to administer the Kissing Test."

"What?" Vi searched her memories for that night but she drew a blank. "Are you sure?"

"You had long brown hair." He ran his palm over her windblown locks. "You were wearing a yellow polo shirt and a blue skirt with matching blue, high top sneakers."

That sounded like the way Violet used to dress. Preppy. Bright colors.

Coop grinned. "And after you kissed me, you blew a bubble with my chewing gum."

Violet gasped, suddenly remembering. "You didn't pass the test."

"No. And I'm not sorry." Coop brushed his nose tenderly across hers before drawing her close. "And if that isn't enough proof of fate, there's something else. This house? The one where Xuri's boat docked? It belongs to my parents."

She gasped once more, wiggling free of his embrace. "Which explains your clean, dry clothes." He was no longer wearing his wet chauffeur suit. She hadn't noticed until now.

"Yes." Coop took her hand. "We're meant to be together, Vivi. You loved Shakespeare enough to make him your life's work.

Trust in his belief in fate." His voice dropped to a whisper. "And if you can't trust him, trust in me and my belief that our love was always meant to be."

Love. For such a short word, it carried powerful connotations. Love. It could change everything for her.

Violet stared into Coop's eyes. He was a playboy, a charmer, from a family that could just as easily make the news as hers could. On paper, he was everything that a Harvard associate professor up for tenure should avoid.

But fate...

And love...

They could be found in Coop's steady, brown eyes.

"I love you, Vivi." Coop gave her hands a gentle shake. "I'm the man who quotes Shakespeare because it's as deeply ingrained in my consciousness as it is in yours. I'm the man who enjoys both a little adventure and a little stability. I'm the man who wants to help people and animals. I'm the man..." He stroked his thumbs over the back of Violet's hands. "...who wants you to be happy and not completely lost in your books 24/7. And I'm the man who knows you aren't happy unless you get uninterrupted time with those very same books. I'm telling you that I know you and you know me. I'm in it for the duration no matter what happens between me and my dad or you and Harvard."

I'm in it for the duration.

I could love this man.

He'd brought Violet smiles and coffee this week, looking past her groggy crankiness. He'd expressed interest in Shakespeare and her grandmother, both of which could be trying. He'd come to her grandmother's rescue and hadn't complained. Nor was he bailing now. He was saying that he'd stick with her no matter what. And she... And she...

Violet felt the same. She loved him.

"Say you believe in fated, true love, Vivi," Coop said softly. "Say it and I'm yours."

The wind had died down. The waves rolled gently to shore.

The moon's glow reached them in their small haven. It was as if the very world around them was waiting for Vi to acknowledge the truth.

"I believe in fated, true love." She was going to have to rewrite her paper, gosh darn it. "And I believe in you, Charles Cooper Pearson the Third. I love you. So very much." Violet reached for him as if she'd been reaching for him forever.

~

"I CAN'T BELIEVE the sun's coming up." Coop walked out of his Hampton's home, one arm draped over Vivi's shoulders. The sun was indeed rising, shining on a day that held the promise of love.

The rest of their group followed them out—Dotty, who'd fallen asleep on the living room couch, Simon and Kelcie, who walked hand in hand.

"Coop?" a masculine voice called to him from near the garage.

Coop slowed. Turned. "*Dad*?"

His father crossed the crushed gravel driveway, looking thinner yet healthier than he had two months ago. His button-down shirt and slacks hung in rumpled, awkward excess. "Was there a party here last night?" He gestured to the catering van that trundled toward the main road.

"Yes." Coop felt the energy drain right out of him because he knew what his father would think—that Coop had hosted the event.

"It figures." Dad came to a stop a few feet away from them. He took his time looking them over.

Coop knew what he'd see – a collection of weary people with rumpled clothes and bags under their eyes. Simon with his food-stained T-shirt. Kelcie with her exercise clothes, faded make-up, and flyaway blond hair. Dotty, also in exercise clothes and with gray hair that practically stood on end. Vivi with her tangle of brown hair, wearing a pair of borrowed flip flops and carrying her high heels.

"You think I arranged this party?" Coop shook his head, trying to shake off the need to defend himself because it would only be a lost cause.

"Are these your parents, Coop?" Dotty asked in a worn-out tone. "I'm not sure I approve of your father's manners."

"Of course, it was you." Dad scowled at Dotty, and then Coop. "Who else would have done it?"

"Me." Coop's mother walked past Dad and hugged Coop. She wore casual, white slacks, a bright red silk blouse, and smelled like roses. "Good to see you, honey. I've been waiting two months for your call."

"Don't make excuses for the boy, Ellie," Dad practically howled. "You weren't even here last night. And he's been here for two months. I can only imagine what the inside of the house looks like."

"Is this going to take long?" Dotty sighed and came to lean on Vivi. "I'm beat."

Coop felt a responsibility to get the elderly woman home. But he still had to defend his honor to his father. He stepped out of his mother's embrace. "I may have been here two months, Dad, but this is the first time I've been to the house. I didn't host a party."

"A likely story," Dad snapped.

"Charles, do you think I need to attend the parties that happen here?" Mom patted Coop's shoulders before turning to face his father with a proud smile on her face. "When we bought this place, you said we could keep it as long as I made the payments. Well, I've never missed a payment yet. I rent out the house and the grounds and I'll have you know, I make a good profit."

A white van with a big sign painted on the side—*Hampton Maid Service*—pulled into the driveway.

"*You* rented the house?" Dad was flabbergasted.

"Yes. We'll talk about this later, Charles." Coop's mother headed toward the front door, digging in her purse, presumably for the keys. "Coop, I'll be expecting you for dinner."

"Yes, ma'am." Coop grinned.

"But he... But you..." Dad was having a hard time finding his bluster. "Coop, I told you to make your own way in the world."

"Hi. Sir?" Vivi waved her hand to get Dad's attention before Coop could continue to engage in the no-win argument. "We had a rough night. Someone stole my grandmother's anniversary ring and it took us until the wee hours of the morning to get it back. We couldn't have done it without your son because it was like the thief vanished into thin air."

That was a Shakespeare quote. Wise move on Vivi's part.

"And I think it was fate that brought us to your house," Vivi continued. "We certainly didn't plan to be here."

"Is that so?" Dad's eyes widened, perhaps because Vivi was dropping hints that she and Shakespeare were good friends.

"I don't know why you insist upon berating your boy." Dotty heaved another weary sigh. "He's been taking care of me all week, working as my chauffeur. He's very responsible and considerate, not to mention patient. I'm told I'm a handful."

Coop and his friends all rushed to reassure her that wasn't true. And then Vivi, Kelcie, and Simon talked on top of one another, each trying to vouch for Coop.

"The door is open, Charles." Mom came back down the steps and hooked her arm through Dad's. "I'm sure there's still a lot to say, but we took a red eye flight and Charles needs his rest."

His father let himself be led toward the door.

"Dad, we have a lot to talk about. But right now, I need to get everybody home and drop off the car to my boss." Without waiting for his father's reply, Coop led his silent band of friends to the Town Car.

"Why do I feel like I've been caught doing something wrong?" Dotty asked as they drove away.

"I'm sorry, Dotty." Coop felt the need to apologize. "My dad has high expectations for me while also having a low opinion of me."

"Don't apologize for his misconception, dear." Dotty had her head hanging out the open rear window. "I enjoyed his surprise when your mother lay claim to the party. His reaction reminded me of my son, Tim. He's a stuffed shirt, too. No offense."

"None taken," Coop reassured her. He reached across the center console for Vivi's hand.

"I should apologize," Vivi said, quietly. "Last night was my fault. If I'd put Grandma Dotty's ring in my purse, our evening would have ended with the first party."

"I still would have wanted my coat," Dotty grumbled.

"Don't apologize, Violet," Kelcie piped up. She sat in the middle seat between Dotty and Simon. "I may have a hangover from whatever someone put in my drink, but last night was one of the best nights of my life. Right, Simon?" She kissed his cheek.

"Right."

Coop drove them home, grateful for their friendship and love, and marveling that he'd managed to find it in the most unlikely of situations.

Later, after Coop had gotten some sleep, he drove the ramshackle pickup to his parents' house and perched on a chair in the living room to have a heart-to-heart with his father.

"I have no interest in the oil business right now, Dad." That much was clear to Coop. "And—"

"I was afraid of that." Anger pummeled his father's words. "I won't support your irresponsible lifestyle anymore."

"I'm not finished." He placed a hand on his father's arm. "I want to make a difference in the world."

"One party at a time, I'm sure." Dad rolled his eyes.

"If you look and listen, you'll see that my heart is on my sleeve." Coop let that Shakespearean reference sink in. "I want to help people start their own businesses."

"Throwing money away at the whim of your friends, no

doubt." But despite his words, there was an absence of anger in his father's tone.

But Coop was tired, not just physically but of the constant struggle to prove himself to the one man who should believe in him. He stood. "If your opinion of me is that low, there's no point in me saying anything else. You can have your credit cards and anything you've bought me." He gestured out the window to the old truck. "I can make it on my own."

His father took in the truck parked outside and then Coop's cheap attire. "I'm listening."

"I've met people here who have big dreams about their future," Coop began slowly. "But they can't make their dreams a reality without risking a roof over their heads. There's Dr. Maggie Summer. She wants to open her own veterinary practice for large animals. It's a capital intensive business start-up given the type of equipment she needs."

Dad's brow furrowed.

Coop hurried on with his examples. "And there's Simon Marchand. You know his family. He wants to start his own high-end restaurant. But he has no equity to secure a loan. And Rafi Moretti, a hard-working horseman who wants to start a horse farm."

His father shook his head. "Why can't these people just go to the bank?"

"You know why," Coop said, using some of that patience Dotty credited him with. "They aren't deemed a good financial risk. They're too young or lack savings or a home to secure a loan." Coop paused, letting that sink in. "I want to start a small business loan and mentoring program, an angel investment firm. I don't want to *give* our money away. And I'd like to have you and other experienced business owners on the board."

"You've thought this through." His father seemed shocked.

"Some," Coop agreed, although he knew there was a long road ahead until his idea was operational. "I'm passionate about helping people. I always have been. And although I know someday I'll run the family fortunes, that day is a long way off. And we're too much alike to work side-by-side every day." The words were still coming out fast, but Coop hoped with sincerity. "I'd like your funding and blessing to run the project. But if you don't approve, I'll find my own backers. If I've learned anything in the past two months, it's that I can make my own way."

"I'd be honored to support this venture of yours." His father beamed at him. "I'm proud of you, son."

Coop couldn't remember the last time his father had smiled at him in such a way. "And there's something else. *Someone* else. I'm going to marry a literature professor. I love her and she..." He gave a little laugh. "She loves Shakespeare."

"Not that it matters if you love each other," Dad said gruffly, standing and hugging Coop.

And Coop couldn't remember the last time that had happened either.

Chapter Fourteen

"I LOVE YOU, BUT I'M NOT GOING TO ARGUE WITH YOU, Shakespeare." Violet crossed her arms over her chest and sat back in her seat in the display area of Summer Diamonds in New York City. She fixed Charles Cooper Pearson the Third with a hard stare, daring him to challenge her.

"I want you to have a diamond that shines just as brightly to others as you do for me." Coop took Vi's hand and slid a ring on her finger, a thick, platinum band with a five karat diamond mounted on it.

"You're too tall to have short man's disease." Vi let her hand drop on the top of the display case as if the diamond was too heavy for her hand to support. Her cousins, who ran the place, sniggered. "This rock says more about you than me or our love."

"Professor Summer, I'm wounded." Coop made a puppy-dog face beneath the brim of his black cowboy hat. They may have been in New York, but true to his word, Coop was a Texan through-and-through. "This is supposed to be a celebration of our love and accomplishments."

She'd recently made tenure at Harvard and his investment firm was going to launch in the new year.

Vi smirked and held her hand toward Zach, who was in

charge of retail operations. "Take it away." While he slid the behemoth ring from her finger, she caught Braydon's eye. He was her cousin who was most like Coop, or at least he was most like Charles Cooper Pearson the Third before he fell in love with Violet. "My cousins should know what type of ring suits me."

"More than your intended?" Coop smirked back.

"Braydon, show me a ring you'd want your fiancée to wear." That command amused her cousins.

Chad, who ran the entire operation now, drew his brothers back to a large box lined with black velvet and filled with shiny things.

"Dotty would approve of that ring," Coop murmured

Grandma Dotty had worn her ring on the catwalk for an up-and-coming designer during fashion week. Dorcas Hepshut claimed to have heard about Dotty's strutting skills from one of Xuri's rejected models.

"I'm setting us up for a happy marriage." Vi drummed her fingers on the display case glass. "I want us to live our lives for ourselves, not striving to be what people think we should be."

Coop took her hand. "That statement just proves you're still the same passionate, vivid woman I fell in love with."

Vi scoffed.

A few feet away, her male cousins were eavesdropping. They began whispering to each other and pointing at rings.

"It's this one," Braydon said with certainty.

His brothers agreed.

And when they presented it to Coop for his approval, he nodded. "It's her." He slid the wedding set on Violet's finger.

The feature stone was amethyst, oval cut. It wasn't too large or too small. Smaller diamonds framed the stone, making it look like a purple-centered daisy. The wedding band crisscrossed the engagement ring band, forming what looked like small leaves.

Vi loved it immediately. She smiled at her cousins and at Coop.

"This is a vivid ring for a vivid woman." Coop stared deep in her eyes. "Did my heart love till now? Forswear it, sight! For I ne'er saw true beauty till this night." His smile was as soft as his words were uttered. "I love you, Vivi. Will you marry me?"

There was no need for him to ask again. But he was a romantic, through and through, and her fate, as evidenced by his quoting *Romeo and Juliet*.

"My answer, Shakespeare, will always be yes." And then, to prove it, she kissed him.

Epilogue

As the youngest sibling, Maggie Summer was used to being last.

Last one to get braces, a bra, and a boyfriend. Last one to earn a driver's license and a graduate degree.

And now...

She stood against the wall at her sister Violet's engagement party in Boston and realized all her sisters were either married—if you counted Aubrey's impromptu foreign ceremony—or were getting married. While Maggie...

Maggie's former fiancé was marrying her oldest sister Kitty this Christmas. And although Maggie no longer loved Beck and had come to peace with the marriage, she had no date.

Violet had taken pity on her and had agreed to fix her up with a prince from a foreign land who was a graduate student at Harvard. But the man was a no show.

Maggie gripped the wilted red rose she'd been holding for the past hour, the sign to her blind date that she was Vi's sister.

She tossed it on a nearby table just as a man came in the door.

His gaze swept the room, caught on the rose, and then lifted to Maggie's face.

He was gorgeous. Clean cut, dark hair. Intense green eyes.

Chiseled cheekbones and regal bearing. He wore a dark suit and tie and hadn't stopped staring at Maggie. That had to mean he was smitten, right?

He was everything a girl in need of a fake boyfriend was looking for to get through two weeks of wedding events.

Want to find out what happens next?

Follow Melinda Curtis to be notified of the release of Maggie's story: *Every Little Kiss.*

Did you read A Kiss is Just a Kiss, the first book in the Kissing Test series?

Don't forget to sign up for Melinda's newsletter on her website and receive free reads.

About the Author

Award-winning, USA Today Bestselling Author Melinda Curtis writes for Harlequin, Grand Central Forever and Caezik Romance as well as being independently published. After much exploration to find her author voice, she now writes mostly sweet romance and sweet romantic comedies. One of her books – *Dandelion Wishes* – was made into a TV movie – *Love in Harmony Valley*, starring Amber Marshall. Melinda has written and sold over 70 books, including several about the Summer family and Grandma Dotty, including the popular Bridesmaid series, now available in audio. In between writing deadlines, Melinda can either be found helping her husband with home remodeling projects, reading, or watching romcoms.

Learn more about her books at MelindaCurtis.com, on Facebook @MelindaCurtisAuthor or on Instagram @MelCurtisAuthor.

Other Books By Melinda Curtis

CHRISTMAS AT THE SLEIGH CAFÉ, A 1ST PERSON ROMCOM FROM THE CHRISTMAS MOUNTAIN SERIES

Can't Hurry Love, Book 1 in the small town, lighthearted, Sunshine Valley series

Dandelion Wishes, now a TV movie "*Love in Harmony Valley*"

Kissed by the Country Doc, Book 1 in the small town Mountain Monroe series

The Wedding Promise, Book 1 in the Bridesmaid romcom series

Discover more titles at on Melinda's website.

www.MelindaCurtis.com

Made in the USA
Coppell, TX
05 April 2023

15272186R00092